HIS LOVE WAS LAW 2

K. RENEE

D1502833

"Savi! Oh my God!" I cried out. I was crawling on the floor trying to make it to my son. The shots ceased, and I hopped up running into the bedroom.

"Savi!" I screamed.

"Mommy!" He was down on the floor screaming and crying. Checking him to make sure he wasn't hurt, I picked him up, holding him tight.

"Mommy is right here baby, are you alright?" I asked him.

"I'm scared, I want my daddy," he cried.

"I know, Baby, but I need for you to be a big boy," I said to him as I heard Tay cursing, and screaming.

"Savi, stay right here, and I will be right back." Kissing him on his forehead, and placing him on the bed as I ran out of the room.

"Tay! Grammy!" I yelled out, as I ran into the kitchen.

"Grammy, are you alright?" Tay asked her, as she helped her get into a seat. Just as I was getting ready to speak the door was being kicked in.

"Tay! Love!" someone called out.

"It sounds like Sin," Tay spoke, as she stopped pacing.

"We're in here!" Tay yelled. She was a complete mess. We were all a mess; those bullets could have killed us, but I'm so grateful that we are all okay.

"Are y'all alright?" he asked as he pulled Tay into him. Clearly, we weren't dead, but we damn sure weren't alright. Somebody decided they wanted to shoot up the block.

"What the hell is going on, who were they after?" Tay asked Sin.

"Listen I'm not sure what the hell is going on, but from the way it looks, they were shooting at this house," Sin expressed.

"Oh my God, who would want to shoot up my house?" Grammy asked as tears continued to fall from her eyes.

"This house! What the hell you mean they were shooting at this house? My grandmother has been on this damn block for forty-five years. Nahh, they had to be shooting at another house and we just got caught in the crossfire," I said to him. I was pissed the hell off, my son, Grammy, Taymar, and I could have been killed.

"I know how it sounds, but most of the bullets hit this house. One of the neighbors said he was standing outside and one of the shooters got out of the car and was shooting into this house. I had just turned on the block when the shots started, but I had no idea that they were hitting this house up. I assumed that it was some street dudes at war, so I got back to avoid getting hit. I will get to the bottom of this, but we have to go. Y'all can't stay here, Ms. Josephine I promise you I will find out who did this," Sin stated.

"Ms. Josephine, the cops are here," Lola from next door yelled inside the house. We all moved outside to the porch.

"Ma'am, I'm detective Daniels, do you have any idea who would want to harm you?" he asked Grammy.

"No sir, I don't, I have been here for forty-five years and never caused harm to anybody. My granddaughters are here visiting from New York, and Miami because my daughter passed away," Grammy said as she held her chest.

"Grammy, are you okay?" I asked her, grabbing her arm to help her sit in the chair.

"I'm fine this shit is just stressful! Who would do something like this to us?" she angrily questioned.

"Sir, we don't know who did this. As you can see my grandmother is highly upset, and so am I. We can't answer any of your questions because we don't know anything," I told them.

"I'm sorry that this has happened. We will investigate this and contact you all with our findings. The officers should be done here soon," Detective Daniels stated.

"Grammy come on and let's pack your clothes. We won't be staying here for a while," I said to her.

"Where is Savion?" Sin asked.

"He's in the bedroom, scared to death," I replied.

"Fuck, I need to call Law!" Sin yelled.

"No! Didn't he just get married? There is no need to bother him with this. I got my son and he's safe," I stated. I was pissed and didn't want to be around Law at the moment. He has a wife; he can make sure she is alright.

"L, I love you and all that good bullshit. But I'm calling my damn brother, he can decide if he wants to leave his wife and come see about his son. That's not a decision you need to make, I haven't said much to you about what you did. But what I will say is, let that man be a father to his kid! You have denied him that right long enough," Sin spoke, and walked away with his phone to his ear.

Chapter Two

LAW

*W*hen we walked in and Jax was fucking Shantel, I lost my muthafuckin mind! I rushed his bitch ass punching him dead in his shit, just as my mom started beating Shantel's ass it was an all-out brawl in this bitch.

"You a fuck nigga! This whole time you have been fucking this hoe ass bitch!" I roared as I continued to beat the shit out of this bitch ass nigga. I didn't give a fuck about him being my dad, that father shit was out the window. This bitch was going to get the beatdown that I have been waiting to unleash on his ass for years.

"Law, I'm sorry it just happened. He means nothing to me, baby!" Shantel screamed, pulling on my arms as I sent blow after blow to this niggas face. I didn't want to hear shit from her hoe ass.

"Bitch don't say shit to my son!" my mom yelled as some of my friends were holding her back, and someone was pulling me off of Jax's pussy ass!

"Naomi, this has nothing to do with you!" Shantel screamed, and my mom was back on her ass beating the shit out of her. Some of my groomsmen moved to pull my mom off of Shantel.

"Don't touch my mother! Let her beat that bitch's ass until she's the fuck tired!" I roared, and they backed up. I was still being held by a few guys because I was damn sure ready to get at Jax's ass again.

"You gone put hands on me over a bitch that gave the pussy up freely!" Jax yelled, as he got up off the floor. I broke away from the hold they had me in and pulled my damn gun out on his ass.

"Say another word and I will blow your fucking brains out all over this fucking room!" I gritted as I held the gun to his fucking head ready to pull the trigger.

"Son! He is not worth the fucking bullet! Let his miserable ass go, you will not go to jail and miss out on any more of your son's life. Fuck them, they can have each other! She ain't got shit anyway that hoe ass nigga is for everybody," my mom spoke rubbing my back to calm me.

"Yeah, listen to your mother, boy!" Jax spat, and I slammed my gun down on his face as blood shot out. Fuck that! I started beating his ass again, and my mom joined in and helped me beat his ass, I was fucking pissed!

"You are dead to me nigga if you ever come around me and my mother. I'm killing your ass!"

"Law, please you have to hear me out!" Shantel ran up and grabbed me.

"Get the fuck off of me! You have one hour to get your shit out of my house, stay the fuck away from me, bitch! If I see your ass again, I'm killing you!" I gritted.

"Yo Law, you need to call Sin, it's an emergency!" Dax said as he walked up to me. I pulled out my phone and I had about ten missed calls from Sin. I dialed his number, he picked up on the first ring.

"Bro, shit is all bad, you need to get over to Ms. Josephine's house. Somebody just shot up her crib! Everybody is okay, they just upset," Sin stated. Walking out of the room, I grabbed my mom's hand pulling her out with me.

"What's wrong?" she asked as we made our way outside with Dax behind us.

"Dax, we need to take your car," I told him.

"Savion, what is wrong with you, son?" my mom questioned again.

"Somebody just shot up Ms. Josephine's house. Sin said everyone is alright, but I need to lay eyes on my damn kid!" I said to her.

"Oh, dear God!" she yelled as we hopped in the car. It took us about twenty minutes to get to Ms. Josephine's house. There were so many people outside, and the cops were here as well. I jumped out of the car and ran inside the house.

"Savi do you have everything packed?" Love asked our son, just as I walked into the bedroom.

"Are you both okay?" I questioned, and Savi jumped up.

"Dad! Somebody shot at us, and I was scared," he cried, and I lifted him into my arms. I was on fucking fire, but I had to be calm in front of him.

"I know Son, I would never let anything happen to you or your mother," I said to him, and looked over at Love. She still hasn't said a word since I walked in the room.

"Okay," he replied.

"Savion, go see your grandmother Naomi, let me talk to your mother for a minute," I told him, and he walked out of the room. Love was throwing clothes in the bag, and I grabbed her hand.

"Love, it's going to be alright," I said to her, and the tears began to fall.

"No, it's not! My son could have been killed! What are you doing here, shouldn't you be on your honeymoon?" she questioned with an attitude.

"The only thing that matters is that you all are alright. I'm sorry that this has happened, and I will get to the bottom of it," I told her.

"We're leaving and going back to Miami, I can't have Savi around this shit!" she stated.

"Listen, I know you're pissed, and so am I. But you have to let me handle this, we don't know what happened here tonight. You all can stay at my apartment, there is no one living there. Just please allow me time to get information on this shit. I need my son right now, I can't let you take him away from me again," I said to her. The anger in my body was rising, and I didn't want to take it out on her. But she was pissing me the fuck off, there is no way I will let her take him from me. If that was her thought process, she needed to change that shit because she would be in the fight of her life. Fucking with me right now is not a good thing to do!

"No thank you, I will figure something out. I will stay in the city, I will more than likely rent something," she shrugged.

"The offer stands if you decide to take it. Come out so that my mom can see that you're alright," I told her, and we went into the living room where everyone was.

"Bruh, let me talk to you outside," Sin spoke. I walked out behind him, and Tay came out as well.

"Tay let me talk to my brother for a minute," he said to her.

"Hell no! If you know something, I want to hear what the fuck you know," she stated, clearly angry.

"Tay give us a minute and I will talk to you about it," he snapped, and she turned and walked back into the house.

"What's up?" I questioned.

"This shit has Tee written all over it, she said to me the other day that my girl would be next. Not only that, on my way here I got a call from Trell. He wanted me to swing by the bar, he said he had some information for me. When I met up with him, he told me that Jax never stopped pushing weight, that Tee was just a front. Jax is the connect and Tee was working for him and fucking him," he stated, and I just looked at him in disbelief.

"Why though? Why would he go through all of this just to make us think he was out! That shit is just fucking crazy!" I replied.

"I know but you know with your pops, he always has a plan for bullshit. He was eating both ways, we were giving him millions just to do nothing. His bitch ass was still collecting our money off the weight we copped off of Tee's ass," Sin spoke.

"I'm telling you this shit right now! Somebody could have killed my kid tonight, and that shit got me ready to murder everybody in this city! If you believe that it was Tee that did this shit, and she is working for Jax. I'm killing them niggas; I almost killed his ass tonight after you left!" I gritted, just thinking about all of this shit had me ready to go to war!

"I know bro, mom pulled me to the side and put me up on that shit. Shantel is a hoe for that shit, and Jax ass should be dead! Ohhhhh Shit, that reminds me, hold up," Sin stated and ran off to his car. When he came back a few minutes later he had an envelope in his hand, handing it over to me.

"What's this?" I asked him.

"When I was leaving the reception to come and get Tay. This chick walked up to me asking if I knew you. Long story short, she said she was Cassy's cousin and Cas came to her and said if anything ever happened to her to deliver this letter to you," he stated. I opened the letter up to see what she had to tell me.

Law,

If you are reading this letter that means that your bitch and father killed me. I know you and Sin don't like me, but I really think you should know what the hell is going on. First of all, your girl Shantel is a muthfuckin' scheming ass hoe! I was drunk and arguing with your dad one day, I left and went back over to his house later that night. I snuck and got a key made so I let myself in. I overheard him talking to two women in his office. I sat and listened as they discussed you, and your brother. The door was cracked and when I peeped in. I saw that one of the women was Shantel, and the other was a girl named Tee that worked for him. They were talking about you having a son, that lived in Florida. I don't know what that was about, but you need to look into that. I ducked off because Tee was leaving but Shantel stayed. Which I thought was strange, which is why I kept listening. Hell, it was strange of her too even be here with them. They began arguing about her still being with you, and then Jax yanked her up and they started kissing. I started to burst in on their ass, but I wanted to see how far they would actually take it. They were fucking right there in his office; I couldn't believe that shit. Your father was a hateful bitch, he only loved your mother. But the fact that she wouldn't be with him, in the way he wanted, infuriated his ass. I think Jax has some mental issues because he couldn't stand the fact that your mother cherished her sons more than him. I even heard him say, that one day when you and Sin were gone, she would come running back to him. With that statement alone y'all need to watch your backs. Believe me, your mother holds all the cards with that man. I just stopped fighting him on it, he took care of me and I was scared to death of him. But back to your bitch! I confronted her about Jax, and she threatened to kill me if I said anything to you. She told Jax that I came to her and beat my ass and threatened to kill me if I talked. Watch your back, Law! They up to some shit, and you and Sin are there number one targets.

Cassy

"What the fuck! So, these muthafuckas want to play with me! They want me to come back to the streets, and body their bitch asses! Well, that's what the fuck is about to happen!" I roared. Sin took the letter and read what the fuck she was saying, and he was now just as angry as I was.

"This shit is fucking crazy; we have to let mom know what's going on. There is more to the story, and we need to figure this out. How did they know you had a son?" Sin questioned.

"I don't know but we gonna find the fuck out!" I gritted. We walked back into the house; it was time that we got them somewhere safe. Sin and I will talk to our mom before the night was over.

Chapter Three

TAY

This shit was all kinds of fucked-up! They thought I was stupid but ain't shit slow about Taymar. That's why Sin wanted to talk to Law by himself, he knew that his ex bitch had something to do with this shit. Grammy's block has always been a cool block, they never have trouble on this block. The people that live over here are older, Love and I don't live here. So, why all of a sudden would her house get shot the fuck up? I don't fight over know damn man, but this bitch is now fucking with my family. We had to call my mom and tell her what was going on. She is coming down in the morning to get my Grammy.

"Tay stop worrying, I told you I'm going to handle this shit," Sin spoke.

"Sin, I'm feeling you and everything but I'm not feeling this bullshit! I know this has that bitch written all over it, all over some dick! My family could have seriously been hurt!" I yelled.

"Tay, what are you talking about? What bitch?" Love asked. She had every right to know what the fuck was going on.

"I think that Sin's ex is the one that shot up Grammy's house. The one that pulled the gun on me, that I told you about," I told her.

"What?! So, this is about a jealous bitch?" Love questioned.

"We don't know that; we are going to check it out. But I believe that it was her, just let us handle this," Sin stated, just as Law walked up.

"Fuck that! You see what the fuck happened here tonight. Stay the fuck away from me! Love, let's get Grammy out of here!" I said and walked off.

"Taymar! Don't fucking walk away from me. I said I will take care of it; I will never let anything happen to you. Your safety and anyone attached to you is my priority right now. Stop doing me like that baby, I can't help that the bitch is crazy!" he grabbed me.

"We need to get Grammy, and Savi out of here. We can deal with this later, I booked us a suite at the Four Seasons," Love said to me. We all grabbed our things and walked out of the house.

"Tay are you coming with me, I need you tonight," Sin stated.

"Nah nigga, I'm going with my family! You need to find

this bitch and deal with her ass! I'm not fucking with you until you fix this shit!" I said turning to walk to the car. Just as I was about to get into the car, I was lifted off my feet and carried away.

"Grandma! Get yo gun, issa good dick nigga invasion!" I yelled, but Grammy was already inside the car and Love was shaking her head. Sin placed me in the passenger seat of his car and shut the door.

"Why are you acting up on me, you know I got this shit and you! If this bitch is the one fucking with you, I'm killing that hoe! Now sit yo sexy ass back and let's go home so I can slide in my shit and calm yo ass down! This shit fucked my ass up, I thought somebody hurt my baby." He smiled.

"Nigga don't be trying to throw me off, by offering good dick, and a smile!" I laughed at him. I was still pissed at what happened, but I knew it wasn't his fault. "Since I know you gonna handle this street shit, I'm going to chill out and let you, do you. How was the wedding? I know that hoe mad because Law came to see about his son, and Love," I said.

"Ohhhh shit, that's right y'all don't know. They got married but Law caught her fucking his dad in their holding room," he said, and I damn near jumped out the window.

"I know you are the fuck lying! Ohhhh this is some ole Jerry Springer type shit right here!" I yelled in disbelief.

"Nahhh, this shit is fucked up. My bro doesn't deserve that shit, he is always getting the short end of the stick and he is such a good dude. Jax and Shantel gonna get what's coming to them you can put that on my life," he snapped, I pulled out my phone to send a text to Love.

Me: CODE MUTHAFUCKIN BLUUUEEE BITCH! But don't call me I will call you in a few.

Love: What happened?!

Me: Bihhh, didn't I say I will call you in a few! Is Law with you?

Love: No, he went to take his mom home and I guess to go check on his wife. He said he will stop by the hotel later to check on us.

Me: Ummmmmmmmmmm ion know about that wife part! But okkkkkaaaayyyy, give me twenty minutes.

Love: You know I hate you right now! Urgghhhhhhh! I burst out laughing because I know her ass was steaming. She wanted the juice, but I couldn't give it to her the way I wanted to deliver it.

"What the hell is wrong with you girl?" Sin asked looking over at me.

"I was laughing at Love; I was checking on them to see if they made it to the hotel yet. I'm worried about them; I think I should've gone with them tonight. My Grammy was really shaken up about all of this," I told him.

"I feel you, babe, Law just texted me to meet him at my mother's house. So, I will drop you off at the hotel and we can spend some time together after I handle this bitch!" He grabbed my hand placing it to his lips.

"Thank you," I smiled at him. I truly liked Sin, but I knew that I had to be careful with my heart. My last relationship nearly took me out loving that piece of shit nigga! I had so much other shit that I was dealing with. Thank god for my mom and dad, they really helped me through that rough time in my life.

My parents were never married but they both did right by me, and I loved the hell out of them. My dad was sick, and he just recently confessed that he believed he had a son. He said he was seeing this chick from the neighborhood, and she just stopped messing with him. He said he saw her about a year later and she had this baby boy with her. She told him that it was her son, and the baby wasn't his and she just walked off. My dad said he thought it was strange because he never questioned her about the child being his. But he did believe the kid favored him, I just felt bad for him. I asked my dad the name of the lady and started doing my research about this chick. If I had a brother out there, I wanted to know about it.

"You alright babe?" Sin asked.

"Yeah, I was just thinking about my dad and that situation I was telling you about," I told him.

"Oh yeah, let me know if you need me to help with anything," Sin stated as he pulled up to the hotel. I'm glad we decided to be with our families tonight.

"I will see you tomorrow! Sin find out who did this shit, I promise you if you don't I will. I may not fight over a man, but I will go to fucking war over my family!" I told him, kissing his lips and stepping out of the car. I texted Love and asked her what room they were in. When she texted back, I hopped on the elevator.

"Tay what are you doing here? I thought you were going with Sin?" Love asked when she opened the door.

"I changed my mind, I needed to be with y'all tonight. But fuck all that other shit, let's talk about the muthafuckin juice I got for yo ass, bihhh! Did you talk to Law about his wedding?" I asked her.

"No, we didn't talk about it at all. Why?" she questioned looking at me all crazy.

"Girlllll, Sin told me that they did get married, but Law caught hoella fucking his daddy, bitchhhhhhhh! Lawwwwd I need me a damn dranky drank on this tea right here!" I told her and went to these good people bar and poured me a damn double-shot!

"Tay are you fucking serious?!" Love jumped up from her seat.

"I swear on Grammy and all the weed in her damn bra! That bitch is fucking dirty, and I swear I'mma whoop her ass for free! If I see her again, it's on sight! He didn't deserve that shit, that's really fucked up!" I told her.

"Damn, now I feel bad for snapping on him!" Love stated.

"Mmmmmmm mmmmmm, don't feel bad for him because that shit will make you vulnerable. He still went ahead and married that hoe; I know you love him. But bitch don't you ever play second best to no damn body! Just don't get caught up, you already know what the dick is hittin for. Well noooo you don't because that was that young twenties era dick you got. His ass probably done improved, and more skillful now that he older! Wheeewww chile, just pray to the good dick gawwds, that they will get you out of a good dick situation!" I said, shaking my head at the thought.

"Taymar! I'm not going to get in a situation with Law," she replied, and I looked at her ass with the side-eye.

"Bitch, he already done had yo ass in the air twice and you parted them damn legs like the red fuckin sea both times! Just make sure Savi around when y'all in the same room. We have to come up with a game plan, now that his ass free to put his dingle in yo muthafuckin puzingle!" I told her and fell out laughing.

"Tay that's not even a damn word!" she laughed.

"Yes, the fuck it is, because I just made it one," I stated.

"I hope they find out if this chick is responsible for what happened. I don't like feeling like this and I need to know that you are going to be safe. Because if it was her, then she is going to try to come for you again," Love stated.

"Love we can't worry about shit we can't control. If it's my time to go, then a bitch gone go out guns blazing! I got this; I'm giving him time to handle this shit as my man. If he doesn't then Tay got it! It's been a long time since we been around each other cuz. I'm not the same Tay, I'm still crazy as hell but I will fuck a bitch up."

Chapter Four

SIN

I know Tee did this shit to Tay, and her family and that bitch is a dead bitch! I don't have to look into shit, because this bitch had the nerve to text me and ask if my bitch was dead! I pulled into my mom's driveway and jumped out of the car. When I walked in the house I could hear mom, and Law talking.

"I'm going to kill this bitch!" I gritted as soon as I walked into the family room.

"Who?" Law questioned as he stood.

"Tee is the one that shot up Ms. Josephine house, this bitch had the nerve to text me saying I could come over and cry over my dead bitch! I'm killing that bitch; on everything I love she gone die!" I roared.

"Yeah, my muthafuckin son could have been hurt or killed.

Not to mention the rest of the ladies, yeah, she gotta die! I said I would never come back to the street life unless some shit popped off with my family! She done woke up the beast and I'm killing anybody in my muthafuckin way! That includes Jax ass, I know he has his bitch ass hands all over this bullshit. If she works for him, that nigga probably set all of this shit in motion," Law spat.

"I can't believe these dirty muthafuckas been on some fuck shit all these years. All because I loved my sons more than his bitch ass and to think I was still fucking his pussy ass! Y'all do what the fuck you have to do concerning these bitches. But I'm going to handle this pussy ass nigga Jax, he knows I have two fucking rules. Don't fuck with my sons, or my muthafuckin money, cause that shit will get your ass killed! I mean I always knew he had an issue with Sin, and I told his ass my son will always come before his ass. So, he tried to clean that shit up, and start helping take care of you. But with Law, he was always pissed that you never took his side and sided with your brother. He never said the shit, you could just see the envy in him all the damn time. But this shit here is crazy as hell!" my mom angrily spoke.

"Man fuck that nigga! I'm gonna see his ass for what the fuck he did to my brother! Believe that shit, ma you need to stay back and let us handle this shit. I don't need you getting hurt," I told her.

"Hell no! I'm in this shit! He out there plottin', and I'm in here plottin; he's a dead nigga! PeriodT!" my mom fussed.

"Something that has been eating my ass alive for the last couple of hours is, how the fuck did they know I had a kid? Shantel acted just as surprised as I the fuck did when I told her about Savion," Law stated.

"It's some bullshit all the way around, but we gonna find the fuck out," I told him.

"Yeah it is, it's getting pretty late and I promised Love that I would stop by and check on them. We need to handle this shit and do it soon, there is no need to drag this shit out. I want the niggas responsible dead. I don't give a fuck who it is!" Law spoke.

"We not gonna be able to get at Tee if she is in her house. I did send Cam over there to check shit out, if she is sending text messages like the one she just sent me tonight, she's not at home. That bitch knows that I would be there in a heart-beat. I'm going to chill here with Ma because I don't trust Jax ass. You handle your business, and we move on these niggas later tonight," I told him, and we dapped each other up. Law gave our mother a hug and walked out. I'm glad we didn't move too quickly I think that hoe was betting on that shit. She can take this shit to the bank and cash that bitch; I'm coming for that ass! I called Tay to make sure they were good.

"Hey," she answered.

"What's up? Y'all good over there?" I asked her.

"Yeah, we good, Savi and Grammy are sleeping, and Love and I are just up talking," she stated.

"Oh okay, I wanted to check on you before I took it down and got some sleep," I said to her.

"Okay, I will talk to you later today." She blew kisses in the phone and hung up. I wanted nothing more but a real shot at loving Tay and showing her that I'm serious about being with her.

Chapter Five

LOVE

ay and I were sitting here having drinks, it was well after midnight and we were just drained from the day's activities. I was worried about my Grammy she has never endured no shit like what happened to us tonight. I'm glad she was going to stay with my aunt down in Virginia for a while.

"Ohhhhh shit, look the investigator sent me all of the information on the lady Jackie Thomas," Tay jumped up all damn hype.

"Tay, who the hell is Jackie Thomas?" I questioned.

"The lady my dad was with back in the day, he believes her son is his. How the hell you forget that quick? We just talked about the shit," she stated, and I laughed.

"You never told me the lady's name, Tay. Anyway, what the

hell does it say? You reading and ain't telling me shit," I looked at her.

"Damn, it says that she gave birth to a son in 1986 at the University of Pennsylvania. She gave birth to a baby boy on November 2nd, 1986, damn it's his birthday. She gave him up to the foster system when he was a year old. Now that's fucked up," Tay fussed. Someone knocked on our door, and I jumped up to answer it. It was Law, and he looked extremely tired.

"Hey, I wanted to stop by and check on y'all before I went home," he stated, as I allowed him to come in.

"Hey Law, ummmmmm, Love can I see you in the room for one minute?" Tay asked.

"Sure, I will be right back," I told Law and followed behind Tay into the bedroom.

"What's up?" I questioned as soon as we stepped inside the room.

"Remember what the fuck I said, you better start praying to the good dick gawwds now! Bihhhhh he looks like he could tear your ass three ways from fuckin Sunday right about now! No matter how bad yo shit jumpin you better lock them legs together and go clink clink on his ass. That's the only way you gonna be safe!" Tay said, and I was bent over in laughter. This girl was crazy.

"Where did they get you from?" I asked her, as I continued to laugh.

"That's the same shit you gonna be asking his ass when he got dick coming out through yo nostrils! That shit is going to be so good, you gonna be like *'where did they get you from.'* He came from the good dick academy bitch, where the rest of them good dick bastards came from!" She laughed, and I was in tears I was laughing so hard at her.

"Tay, I got this!" I told her.

"Okay, *I got this,* I don't want to hear shit from you when he gets yo ass!" she stated and plopped down on the bed. I walked back out to talk to Law, I wondered if he was going to tell me about what happened at his wedding.

"I'm sorry about that," I said to him as I took a seat on the couch next to him.

"Mmmmm, mmmmm, outta all the seats in there, you sit next to his ass. Grammy Love gone have dick hanging out her nose in about three point five seconds don't come out the room!" Tay yelled out and both me and Law turned in the direction of her voice, but she must have jumped back. I was so damn embarrassed; I could only shake my head.

"That girl is something special." He smiled.

"Yeah, but I love her," I spoke.

"Love, I'm sorry about what happened. I'm in a place where I'm ready to murder every nigga on the streets over this shit. I never want to see you and my lil' guy in any danger. I promise I'm going to take care of this, we already know who's involved," he stated.

"I know, Tay told me about the chick. You should be with your wife instead of being here with me," I said to him, just to see if that would spark the conversation.

"Nah, I'm cool on her, it's true she is my wife but not for

long. I caught her fucking my pops at our reception," he stated, rubbing his hand over his face.

"What?! I'm sorry to hear about that. How are you feeling about it?" I questioned.

"Numb, the signs were there, and I just walked all around that shit! I was so focused on the situation with you and Savion that nothing else really mattered. It's like this bitch wasted years of my life that I will never get the fuck back. To find out that this bitch has been fucking with that nigga for a while now is crazy to me. But I will be good, it's nothing that I won't get over," he stated.

"I feel bad that you are going through this, but if you ever need to talk, I'm here," I told him, and I meant that. Tay was right, even though I loved him and have all of these feelings for him. He didn't choose me; he married this woman and I'm going to try and move on with my life. But, I'm okay with being friends with him, we do have a son together.

"Thanks that's good to know, I'm going to get out of here and let you get some rest. I will check on you later today," he stood to leave, and I got up to walk him to the door.

"Get some rest," I said to him, and he just stood there staring at me. He pulled me in for a hug, and I didn't reject him because I felt like he needed it. When he turned me loose, he smiled and walked out the door. This was going to be a hard battle to fight, but I had to stand strong.

Chapter Six

LAW

The only thing on my mind was murder. I still can't believe the shit that fucking happened at my so-called wedding. I put all my trust into a nothing ass bitch! My pops can best believe he hasn't seen the last of me. But first, we need to see this Tee bitch. My son is my number one priority and to think that this bitch went and shot up a house that he was in. Nah, that shit doesn't work like that with me, that bitch will be eating my fucking bullets in the next twenty-four hours. I pulled up in my driveway and I couldn't believe my eyes, I know damn well this bitch wasn't in my house. Her car was parked in the driveway like the shit belonged here. I jumped out of my car quick as hell, when I stepped inside, she was sitting in my family room.

"What the fuck are you doing in my house?! You got a

minute before I fill your ass up with bullets, get the fuck out!"
I roared.

"Savion, I need you to let me explain, please! We're
married, you have to at least let me explain!" she cried, gripping her up by her damn neck with my gun pressed to her
face.

"Explain what exactly, bitch! Explain that your hoe ass was
fucking my pops at our fucking reception! By the way, we
never signed the marriage license with the pastor you were
too busy getting fucked! I called the pastor and told him to
rip that shit up. If you don't get the fuck out of my house, I'm
murdering your ass and burying you in my back yard! Don't
test my muthafuckin gangsta, bitch!" I gritted.

"You can't kill me, I'm pregnant with your baby!" she
stated, and I let out a thunderous laugh. This bitch is simple
if she thought I was going to believe the bullshit she was
talking right now. I sent my mom a text and something hit me
at the mentioning of her being pregnant.

"How long have you known about my son?" I questioned
her as I pushed the gun deeper in her face.

"Wha...What are you talking about?" she questioned.

"Bitch! How fucking long?" I asked her again.

"I don't know what you're talking about, I found out when
you told me. Savion, I'm having your baby, it's not Jax's baby!"
she screamed, and I shoved her down on the couch. I didn't
say shit to her, I was waiting for my mom to show up. I just
sat there and mugged the shit out of her ass, while she kept
trying to talk to give her bullshit explanation.

"Shut the fuck up! You're sitting here crying these bullshit ass tears, bitch fuck you, you can choke on them damn tears for all I care." About fifteen minutes later, I heard my mom opening the door.

"Law!" she called out.

"I'm in here, mom!" I yelled.

"What is she doing here?!" Shantel barked.

"Bitch you are in no position, to be questioning shit up in here! You better shut the fuck up, before I beat that ass again!" my mom spat.

"Did you get what I asked you to get?" I asked her, and she nodded that she did. I pulled Shantel up grabbing the bag out of my mom's hand and pushed her to the guest bathroom.

"What are you doing?" she asked, looking confused.

"Piss on this fucking stick! If you're pregnant we about to find out right now!" I roared.

"I'm not pissing on this," she griped, and I pulled my gun up to her head once again. She snatched the box nervously and proceeded to do what I asked. We waited until the pregnancy test results appeared on the stick. This bitch was lying, and the tears were really falling.

"You already know what the fuck it says, what you thought by telling me you were pregnant that I would forgive you, and take you back? Start fucking talking! How long have you known about my son?!" I asked her ass.

"Okkaayyy, okay! I've known for years, Teana that works for your father. Zion's is her half- brother! Jax wanted to see you hurt, and he asked Zion to make sure that he kept your son away. I didn't want you to find out about your son, because I knew that meant Love would come back in your life. Jax hates you and Sin, his hatred got worse when y'all took over and tried to cut him out of the dope game. He talked about it all the time. The shit with me and Jax just happened, and after that, he held it over my head and threaten to tell you. So, I kept seeing him, because I never wanted you to find out!" she cried grabbing on to my shirt. I pushed her ass off of me, and pulled the trigger letting shots off into her chest! Fuck that heartless, lying bitch! My mom came running into the bathroom.

"Son come sit down, I need you to get your mind right. This bitch was fucked up, and so is your snake ass daddy," she said, as she picked up the phone and called Sin to come over and bring the cleanup crew with him.

Chapter Seven

TAY

My mom had come and picked up Grammy, and Savi was hanging with his grandmother Naomi. He was excited about that, she said she wanted to give Love a break. I had all the information on the guy that could possibly be my dad's son. But I was so nervous about going to the address that I had for him. I just felt so strongly about doing this for my dad, and me too. If I had a brother out there, I wanted to know about him. I paid this investigator a lot of money in the past few months to make this happen. I figured dealing with this, would take my mind off of this bitch Tee. I was serious when I told Love, shit with me have changed over the years. My ex was into a lot of street shit, and I had to toughen up when I met him. There was always somebody trying him, and me.

"Tay, what's wrong?" Love asked.

"I'm just trying to decide if I'm going to go see him. I really want to, but what if he doesn't want to hear what I have to say?" I questioned her.

"We won't know until we try," Love stated, and I looked at her.

"What do you mean we? Are you going with me?" I asked excitedly.

"I would never let you do something like this alone. Come on let's go meet your potential brother," Love said, and we jumped up to get ourselves together. About an hour later we were in the car, I put the address in the GPS as we were on our way. He lived out in Conshohocken, so we jumped on the highway. We were about five minutes away from his house and damn he must have some money. Because these damn houses were fucking beautiful and huge! When we pulled up to the address the gate was opened, so we just pulled in the driveway.

"Are you ready?" Love looked over at me. I blew out a breath, and we got out of the car. I made sure I had all of the information that was sent to me so that he could have proof. I went down to the hotel computer room and printed every-thing out this morning. I walked up the steps and rang the doorbell, it took a few minutes. A beautiful woman greeted us when she opened the door.

"Hey, can I help you?" she questioned.

"Hello, my name is Taymar, I'm looking for a Gabriel Thomas," I said to her, and she cut her eyes at me.

"What exactly do you need with my husband?" the lady questioned with a bit of an attitude.

"Well if you drop......." I was cut off by Love. Because I was about to let it rip on her ass.

"Excuse me, we're looking for Gabriel because we believe that he may be her brother," Love told her. She seemed shocked, and then turned to look in the house and then back at us.

"What, how do you know that for sure?" She looked from me to Love.

"Because I have all of the records, from his birth. I know that he went into foster care when he was a year old. My father believes that he is his son, and I wanted to find him," I told her.

"Gia, why the hell you got the door wide open letting the fuckin devil in here. It's hot as hell outside....." some guy yelled as he came around the corner.

"Oh shit," Love whispered because this man looked like he could be my damn twin.

"Who y'all?!" he asked.

"Babe, I think we need to sit down and talk to these ladies. Don't you think she favors you?" Gia asked him.

"Hell nawl! She doesn't look like my ass! Tell yo mama to go find the nigga that really got her ass pregnant cause it wasn't my ass! I can't even have kids I got fixed when I was two years old, and I ain't got no damn money!" he stated and walked away. Love burst out laughing, and I was the hell stuck. He thought I was coming here to tell him he was my daddy.

"He sounds just like your ass, Tay," Love stated, and Gia was shaking her head.

"Y'all come on in, and get out of this heat," Gia stated, and all of a sudden Gabriel was back.

"Hold the hell up, they can't just walk in here. We don't know what the fuck they got on them! Do y'all got roaches or rats at y'all house? Like how often do y'all exterminate? Do y'all have raccoons in yo back yard or snakes? Are you pure, saved, sanctified, and filled with the holy ghost or are y'all like the spawns of satan? Let me go get my damn kit, I gotta check y'all out before you come up in here!" he blurted out as he walked away for a few minutes and came back with a bag in his hand. This nigga pulled out one of those forensic UV lights, and turned the lights off and started running it over my hair and clothes.

"Nigga what the fuck are you doing?! I'm so confused right now. We don't have any of that stuff, who the fuck walks around with roaches on them?" I questioned, as Love and I stood there with our mouths agape.

"It's a long story," Gia stated.

"This nigga weird as fuck, I think I should have left his ass where he was at. Daddy would just have to die wondering. Fuck that! when he dead it ain't gone matter no damn way. I'm just gonna tell his ass, the kid wasn't his. Because this nigga is certified, Ion even want this no mo! Fucka brother,

I'm cool by myself," I whispered to Love, and she burst into laughter.

"Y'all, come on in, my husband has issues with bugs, and he believes that everybody that comes in his house should be checked," Gia said, as we walked into their beautiful home.

"Gabe, she really needs to talk to you," Gia told him.

"Alright, damn! What was yo mama name? Because I'm telling you now. I only fucked with women that had names like Taquashia, Mercedes, and Zamaneisha and shit like that. Gia was the only plain name I fucked with. So, that should tell you if I'm yo daddy or not," he said, and Love burst out laughing.

"Gabe, I'm not here because I think you're my dad. I'm here because I think you're my brother," I told him.

"Mmmmmm, mmmmm hell nawl! Ion need one of them either, they seem like they too damn expensive. Quad sister always got her damn hand out, and every year her ass want a new car. Nope, not me, fuck that! Return to fuckin sender! Besides, I got a sister already her name is Ava!" he stated, and Love was literally bent over.

"Gabe!" Gia yelled.

"Gia! I done told you and Truth about yelling my damn name," he fussed.

"Look I'm not here to take the place of anyone. Here is the information I have on you," I said handing him the folder. He took it and sat down at the table, Love and I sat as well.

"So, this Jackie person that gave birth to me, is she your mother as well?" he questioned.

"No, my father and her were seeing each other back in the day, and he said that he believed that the baby she had was his. He said he asked her, and she denied it, but you looked like him. He is sick, and I wanted to find you for him. Because it's been killing him for years to know if you were really his child," I said to him.

"Ion really need another daddy, I got one of those already. He didn't do a good job at raising my ass, but he mine. This nigga should have been looking for my ass before Truth got his hands on me. Maybe I would have turned out different!" he fussed.

"I just wanted you to know what I found out, and if you're interested in finding out the truth about all of this. My number is in the folder. It was nice meeting you both," I said, getting up and rushing out with Love behind me.

"Tay, I think he was joking around with us, he acts exactly like you. I don't think he was rejecting you.... Ummm, Tay you see that truck, I think that truck was behind us on our way here," Love stated. I turned in the direction of the gate, It was a black SUV parked at the gate. The window rolled down and gunfire sounded off, Love and I immediately hit the ground. Gabe came running out shooting back, I heard screeching tires and the gunshots finally ceased.

"Y'all alright?" he questioned, as he helped me up.

"Love are you okay?" I asked her.

"Yeah, what about you?" she questioned nervously.

"Gabe, what the hell is going on?" Gia was at the door

with a gun in her hand. *Damn who are these people? I thought to myself.*

"Y'all come back in the house, I think we need to have a damn talk," Gabe stated and waited for us to walk inside.

"I'm sorry, I didn't mean to bring trouble to your home. I'm pretty sure that was meant for me," I told him.

"What the fuck are you into so bad, that somebody wants to kill you in broad daylight?" he asked me, he was clearly pissed.

"I'm dating this guy and the girl that he was messing with before me. She wants me dead, she shot up my grandmother's house last night. They must have been following us all this time, but we didn't know it. I've never had these types of problems before," I said to him.

"You mean to tell me, shorty trippin this hard over a nigga?! Is this dude in the street?" he asked.

"Yes," I whispered.

"Well, we have a bigger problem now, because this bitch shot at my damn house! My muthafuckin kids are in this house and my damn wife! I don't play those types of games, so somebody gonna die fucking with mine! I need everything you have on this bitch, and if you don't know anything you need to call this nigga and get it! Better yet take me to this nigga you fucking with, he gone give me what I need!" he roared, and I just nodded. Grabbing his phone, he dialed a number.

"Yo Quad, I'm going to send you an address, I need you to meet me there," he told the guy and ended the call. He passed me his phone and I put my grandmother's address in and hit send. I didn't know if Sin would be angry about me giving out his address. Love and I walked to the car and Gabe jumped in his car to follow us.

"I can't believe this bullshit happened!" I screamed out, as I sent Sin a text telling him to meet us at Grammy's house in thirty minutes.

"This shit is getting out of hand, and I really think we should go back to Miami until they fix this shit. Somebody could get killed, and this girl is crazy. She followed us to his house and didn't give one fuck about it," Love stated. She was right, they really needed to handle this shit. But I do know this, Tay not running from this hoe, it's time to meet this bitch head-on. I must say I feel kind of good, having my maybe brother there to back me up. He seems like he about that muthafuckin life!

Chapter Eight

SIN

*L*aw and I were at my mother's house, we decided to stay here after all of the bullshit that happened with Shantel. That bitch was fucking crazy as hell to even be in the house waiting on Law. Then on top of all of that shit, sit and tell a muthafuckin lie to try and get back in. My mom went and picked my nephew up from Love this morning, and all you could hear was his laughter through the house. I walked downstairs, and Savion was playing with his dad. It was amazing to watch the two of them, the love was evident between both of them. He loves that little boy, I just feel bad for him, all the shit that he has been hit with through the years. I had to go meet Tay, and Love to see what the hell is going on. That text she sent said it was urgent, and she couldn't talk.

"What y'all doing?" I asked.

"Playing, do you want to play with us uncle Sin?" Savi asked.

"I have to make a run, but I promise unc gone spend some time with you. We gonna hang out and play some games," I told him.

"Okay," he replied.

"Bruh, you want to take this ride with me? I got a call from Tay and L. They said it was urgent," I said to Law, and he immediately stood.

"What's up with them?" he questioned.

"Don't know, but we need to go now," I told him as I headed for the door.

"Savi, go into the kitchen and hang out with your grand-mother. I will be back later, and we can hang out then," Law spoke.

"Okay, I love you, daddy," Savi responded and ran off. We hopped in the car and headed to Ms. Josephine's house. About thirty minutes later we pulled up on her block. Tay and Love were standing by Love's car, talking to two niggas. She was gonna make me fuck her lil' ass up, all up in some nigga's face.

"Yo that dude looks familiar as hell," Law stated, as we jumped out the car.

"What's up, and who these niggas?" I asked walking up on them.

"Nigga, you might need to go back to the car and retry the way you walk up on a nigga with all that aggression. We not here for all that shit!" This dude standing next to Tay stated.

"Yo who the fuck you talkin to like that?! Nigga, I will--" I was cut off, by Tay yelling my name and stepping in between us. When she faced me and was standing next to the nigga with all the heart, I couldn't help but notice that they looked like damn twins.

"Sin cut all of that shit out! This is Gabe and his friend Quad, Gabe is possibly my brother that I was telling you about," Tay stated, and I calmed the hell down.

"Law what's up dude, it's been a minute!" Gabe said to my brother.

"What's up man, I have been sitting here racking my fuckin brain trying to figure out if that was you. Q what's up bro?" Law greeted both guys.

"I've been coolin, bruh! We gone have to link up soon, I need some more ink on me," Quad stated.

"Y'all know I got you, damn it's a small world. This is my brother, Sin. We got some issues so we just a lil' tight right now," Law stated.

"My bad, I'm glad she found you, man," I said to him, and we dapped it up.

"It's all good, but it seems that we have a problem. Somebody followed them to my house, and opened fire on them in my damn driveway!" he stated.

"What the fuck?! That bitch gotta die right fuckin now! L and Tay y'all cool?" Law questioned.

"Tay, you good baby?" I asked, pulling her in for a hug.

"Nah! I'm not the fuck good! I told you to fix this shit if you not I will!" Tay yelled.

"Pipe down lil' gangsta, if you're my lil' sis I can't have you out here going to war," Gabe spoke, and Tay nodded.

"Taymar I got this shit!" I roared.

"Nigga if you had it, the bitch wouldn't have had a second chance at trying to kill me!" she stated, pissed the fuck off. She was right I shouldn't have waited; Tee is not stable, and we should have taken care of her ass last night.

"Love, I need for you and Tay to go chill with my mom. You all will be safe there, and we will see y'all once this shit is handled. Tay don't worry that bitch will be dead by the end of the night!" Law told them.

"Okay," Love replied.

"I want to go with y'all," Tay spoke.

"Nah, you need to sit this out," I told her, there was no way I was letting her go with us.

"Let her rock, the girl was trying to kill her, and If she wants to rock out with us, let her do it," Gabe spoke, but this nigga was trippin. I wasn't putting my girl in the line of fire, fuck that!

"Bruh, I'm not putting her in the line of fire, shit can go bad and she get caught up. That shit will be on me, and I can't let that happen," I said to him.

"Looks to me like you already put her in the line of fire, and she will never get caught up with me there," this nigga spoke.

"If something happens to her I'm fucking you up!" I told him, and I meant that shit.

"That will never happen, let's go!" he stated.

"Sin I will be fine, I promise I can handle myself," Tay said to me.

"Just let her go," Law spoke.

"Tay be careful, I know I can't stop you," Love told her.

"I'm good, boo." She smiled at Love.

"We need to go, I'm tired of this bitch and my trigger finger is ready to off this hoe!" Law stated. Love got in her car and pulled off, Gabe and Quad followed behind us. I called Cam to have him and Zeno meet us at the warehouse where we always met up with Tee. I also sent Steve over to my moms, to make sure they were cool until we got back. It took about twenty minutes to get to the warehouse. There were a few trucks parked outside, I'm hoping this bitch was here. I popped my trunk and press the button so that the base of my trunk would rise up. Law Grabbed two AK's and walked off, my brother was no joke when he was pissed the fuck off. I gave Tay a gun, and she immediately walked behind Law.

"Well damn, I see you can handle more than a tattoo gun, nigga," Gabe laughed. The door to the warehouse was opened, and we walked in. There was nobody in the room, all of a sudden, Tee's ass came out clapping.

"I see you came up in here mad, and you bought your bitch! What, you thought I was gonna be running from you? Bosses don't run boo, I let your bitch live! I just wanted to scare her ass for a little while. This should teach you not to lie down with a boss bitch and then try to play her!" she stated calmly.

"Bitch, do you see me scared, I'm pissed the fuck off. But

you gonna learn today about fucking with, Tay!" Taymar yelled.

"Awww the bitch got a lil' heart, but bitch don't fuck with me the next time I won't miss," Tee said to Tay.

"You are one delusional bitch! I was never yours, I fucked you!" I roared.

"Man fuck all that bitch; we don't play that fuck shit! You don't go shoot up nobody's fucking house for the hell of it!" Law yelled as he lifted his gun.

"Hold the fuck up! Teana, you the fucking one that shot up my crib today?" Gabe asked her, as he began pulling shit out of a duffle bag.

"Ga..Gabe...Ummm what are you doing here?" she nervously asked.

"Nah bitch! I'm the one asking the fucking questions!" Gabe roared.

"You know her?" Law questioned.

"Yeah, we know this hoe! She is the conniving bitch that tried to trap Truth back in the day. We heard she been running around trying to help that nigga Jax from the west-side out. They were stepping on some of the niggas that we supply territory," Gabe stated, and Law and I looked at each other, just as Cam and Zeno came walking in.

"Jax is my pops, but that nigga got an expiration date too!" Law told Gabe.

"Say less!" Gabe replied.

"Law you need to watch your back, while you up in here talking that shit! You're just mad because my lil' brother took your bitch and raised yo bastard ass son! You can thank your daddy for that shit! By the way, I see why you mad about Shantel she did have some tasty pussy. Ohhhhhh you didn't know! We were all fucking each other, Shantel's been in my bed so many nights, I can't even count! Jax should have just killed y'all bitch asses a long time ago. But nooo, he wanted to break you niggas down and watch y'all suffer. I must say we played all y'all asses and your bitch ass mama too!" Tee stated, and I was ready to kill this bitch! Law rushed over to her gripping her in the air by her neck. Her crew came rushing out with their guns drawn.

"Oh damn! Now that's some cold shit right there! Mmmmm, mmmmm, bitch don't you know you need to shut the fuck up sometime! Especially when you got a crazy nigga with a loaded AK, holding you in midair! Damn you still slow as hell!" Gabe said to her.

"You need to put her the fuck down nigga!" Tee right hand Blue yelled out to Law, and I sent a shot to her head and silenced that bitch forever. I decided that my brother could kill this bitch, and that would be satisfaction enough for me.

"Jax bitch ass is next, and if your brother ever tries me, he will join y'all asses!" he roared, as he filled her ass up with bullets as he held her in the air. The rest of Tee's crew let off shots, and we were laying their asses down. This nigga Gabe had some big ass shit in his hand that was shooting out fire, and that shit was flaming these damn niggas the fuck up. One of them tried to sneak up on Gabe, but Tay got the drop on that nigga! Damn, I guess I underestimated her ass and she was ready for this shit. These niggas were in here on fire, I mean literally on fucking fire!

"Damn, that bitch was dumb as hell, I guess she had faith in her crew that they could boss up and take us out," Quad spoke.

"Nigga, who shoots fire in a gunfight?!" Tay asked Gabe, as she burst into laughter.

"I do! That shit was cold, huh? I like how you got the drop on that nigga. I got something for you, hold on," Gabe told her, and went to his bag and pulled out some damn honey buns.

"Hell yeah, we got snacks!" Tay clapped, and they both sat on a table swinging they damn feet, eating fucking honey buns.

"Y'all know these niggas is on fire and dead in here, right?" I questioned shaking my damn head.

"Can we have our maybe sister, and brother bonding time, please and thank you!" Gabe spat, as he and Tay high fived each other.

"This the shit that we've been dealing with for years," Quad said, shaking his head.

"Now that this shit is over, I need to get back to my family. Taymar I will call you in a couple of days. Law we gone hit you up soon, take it easy bruh," Gabe said, as he and Quad dapped us up and left.

"Yoooo did she say she was fucking Shantel?!" I asked Law, we both were standing there puzzled as fuck. Shantel was just one nasty hoe, damn everybody was fucking everybody! This shit was crazy!

"I don't even want to talk about that shit right now! If I could wake that bitch from the dead I would, and then kill her ass all over again! Fuckkkkkkkkkkk!" Law roared.

"Cam sweep this place; I think this is where Jax holds his drugs! If you find anything you know what to do, hit me up and let me know what you find!" I told him, and Law and I left the warehouse. On the ride back to our mother's house Law was quiet, and I just left him alone. Jax was just a low life piece of shit, and he was next.

Chapter Nine
LOVE

I was just in shock, all of the shit that has happened in the last twenty-four hours had my head spinning. I was at Ms. Naomi's house waiting to hear from the guys. I was nervous and worried about their safety. I can understand why Law is so angry, hell I'm angry too. This girl could have killed me and Tay today, we wasn't shielded by a house to take cover.

"Love don't worry they are going to be just fine," Ms. Naomi said, as she checked on the fried fish she was cooking.

"Grandma, are we still making brownies?" Savi asked his grandmother. I love the way he has grown so attached to his grandmother. He begged me this morning to come over to her house and she was more than happy to pick him up.

"Yes, baby, as soon as you eat your dinner," she told him.

"Is there anything I can do to help?" I asked her.

"Just get the plates out of that cabinet for me. Dinner is ready and I'm going to fix y'all plates," Ms. Naomi stated.

"Urgghhhh I'm so tired of waiting, I need to know that they are alright," I blurted out, I was really irritable and frustrated.

"Love come sit down and eat your food. They are fine if I don't know anything else in this fucked up world. I know that my sons are alright, and that means that Tay is alright as well," Ms. Naomi stated. We were sitting at the table talking and eating dinner when we heard Sin call out for his mom. I jumped up from the table and rushed into the family room. Law was pacing back and forth, and Sin pulled his mother to the side for a private conversation. I looked over at Tay, and she was shaking her head.

"What the fuck did you just say?!" Ms. Naomi questioned, as she looked back and forth from Sin to Law. I walked over to Law because he looked as if he was ready to burst in flames.

"Law," I softly called out his name.

"Love, hunny, he will be alright," Ms. Naomi said to me, as if she wanted me to leave him alone. But I was worried about him, I had to try and calm him down. I stepped in front of him and grabbed his hand.

"Law, do you need to talk?" I asked him, and he stopped pacing.

"NO!" he gritted, and I let his hand go. I walked away to go and find my son; I don't know what happened. But I know he wasn't going to start disrespecting me again.

"Love, sis, please just give him a break. Don't hold this

against him, we found out some fucked up shit and he needs time to process this shit. He will talk to you about it soon enough I'm sure," Sin said, and I nodded my head trying to fight back the tears that were threatening to fall.

"Okay," I responded.

"We have to make a run, and my mom needs to come with us. I need y'all to chill here until we get back, we should only be a couple of hours. One more thing, do you know this person?" he questioned, pulling up a picture of Teana.

"Yes, that's Teana, she's Zion's sister. How do you know Teana?" I asked him, confused that he knew her.

"This is Tee, she's the one that shot at y'all. It seems that Zion's motives for marrying you was because of some shit that has to do with Jax. I will have more information for you when we get back," Sin said, as he went to talk to Tay. A few minutes later I walked back into the family room. Ms. Naomi came down the stairs and walked out with her sons behind her.

"Shit is fucked up, L. I will tell you all about it later," Tay said, and I shrugged. I was still stuck on the shit Sin said about Zion and his sister. *What the fuck!*

Chapter Ten
LAW

We pulled up to Jax's house, I refuse to call his pussy ass nigga my pop. I jumped out before the car could even stop moving good. Sin and my mother were running behind me, I had already kicked his damn door in. He was running downstairs with his gun in hand, when he noticed that it was me, he dropped it to his side.

"Nah you might want to keep that shit up because one of us is going to die tonight!" I roared.

"Nigga, I'm not going to let you keep putting your hands on me. I fucked Shantel, so the fuck what! Grow some balls and get over the shit, she was never your woman anyway!" he yelled, and I moved to his ass so quick. He raised his gun and pointed it to my head, just as my mother screamed. When he noticed her standing there, he lowered the gun and I tried to break that niggas muthafuckin jaw.

"Savion, stop baby!" my mom spoke, as Sin pulled me off of him.

"How could you do your son like that? You piece of shit ass, nigga! Look at all the deceitful shit you've done to him! You knew that he had a son out there, yet you hated him so much that you said nothing. Then you fucked Shantel, just to hurt him. For what?! So, you could see him break! What kind of man are you? I will tell you what kind of man you are, you're nothing but a bitch made nigga!" my mom screamed at his ass. The only reason I calmed down is that I knew she had to get this off of her chest. But that nigga won't be walking out of this shit alive. Sin already put the text out for the cleanup crew to come.

"You couldn't even love me right, because of these niggas. I tried to marry you years ago, but you felt that I didn't love that bitch of a son you had enough," he spoke.

"Call me another bitch, and you gone eat these bullets as yo last muthafuckin supper, pussy ass nigga!" Sin gritted.

"He was my son! You damn right, I will always love my children before any nigga! I would never fucking marry a man that can't accept my children!" my mom screamed.

"He wasn't my fucking kid, so why should I have given a fuck about him! My own son turned against me because of his brother. So, I said fuck him! If he wasn't with me, he was against me. I hated you, and I still hate your bitch ass. Yeah, I fucked your bitch every chance I got! You were too busy opening your businesses, not giving her the attention she needed. Don't worry your pops kept that pussy right for you.

Fuck being loyal to a nigga that wasn't loyal to me. She loved every minute of that shit, fucking her at your wedding was the best part of my get back. Don't let her fill your head with lies, Shantel was never going to stop fucking me. I'm the one that made my son, Zion, marry Love!" he roared, and I let off a shot into his arm.

"Mom, you need to hurry the fuck up! I'm trying to be patient, but I want to kill this bitch so bad my dick fucking aches!" I gritted, as he held onto his arm.

"What, son?!" Sin asked, shocked at the revelation.

"You had another fucking son?! You one nasty cold son of a bitch, I can't believe that I still fucked you," my mom said to him.

"Ohhhh I got all of your attention now, huh? Yeah, Zion, is my son! I knew he was fucking with Love, he told me all about her. When Naomi called and said that this nigga had fallen in love with, Love, and that I needed to come over and talk to him. Love was already in Miami with, Zion, I'm the one that suggested he should marry her right away. When he called me and told me months later that Love was pregnant by you. He tried to talk her into getting an abortion, but she wouldn't do it. It helped that Love wanted to hide her son from you. I told him to do whatever it takes to keep her from telling you. When Zion met you at the school, he knew then that he was your brother. He wanted to be down so bad, he would do anything to make me proud of him. That made it so much easier for me to pull him in...." he was talking but was cut off by Sin.

"How is he your son, when Tee was his sister and you were fucking her?" Sin asked.

"They had the same mother different fathers; Zion's mother couldn't stand Love. So, keeping Love in the dark was easy to do. As far as Tee goes, once I dug inside that pussy, she was down for whatever." He burst into laughter, there was nothing funny about this shit. Love thought the shit with her, and Zion was real, I'm going to kill that nigga.

"This nigga is sick! You fucked the mom and then years later you get with the daughter. Ma, say what the fuck you need to say because we ready to off his pussy ass!" Sin told her.

"You did all of this because you couldn't have me?" Ma questioned with tears falling from her eyes.

"Yes, you pushed me to the side for these niggas, and then they tried to come up and push me out of the game! Some shit that I started, and they thought they were just gone push me out! Fuck both of you, niggas! I have a son that will do what the fuck I need. I don't give a fuck about you and I damn sure don't need you!" he roared, and my mom lifted her gun and sent two shots to his head. While Sin, and I lit his chest up so bad the bitch opened up. I took the gun from my mother's hand as she broke down in a fit of tears.

"I'm so sorry, son. I can't believe a parent would ever treat their child like he has done. The hatred that he had for you is just unreal to me, I'm so sorry to the both of you. I can't believe that I had a nigga like that around my kids, hating on them all these years," she cried into my chest.

"Mom, this is not your fault and we're not gone let you sit here and blame yourself for this dude being a fucked-up individual," Sin told her, and he was right.

"Mom, I would never blame you for any of this. Don't you ever apologize to us again about this nigga!" I said to her and kissed her on the cheek. The crew was outside, and Sin let them in to clean this shit up.

"Sin, I need you to drop me off to my penthouse, I'm going to be staying there until I can sell my house and buy another one," I told him. There was no way that I was going to stay in that shit that I shared with Shantel. All the shit that we found out today, I was just mentally drained. Damn!

Chapter Eleven

TAY

*I*t's been a few days since I talked to my dad. I needed to check in on him to make sure he was feeling alright. I decided to keep what I had found out about Gabe to myself until we knew for sure. Gabe is pretty cool; I think we will have a lot of fun together. I must admit that Love was right, we do act so much alike. We both just said whatever that came to mind, he was just a tad bit crazy. I heard the door open and Ms. Naomi and Sin walked in the house, I jumped up and ran over to Sin.

"Is everything alright?" I asked, because Ms. Naomi looked as if she had been crying.

"Where is Law, is he okay?" Love asked.

"He's fine, he went to his penthouse," Sin told her.

"I'm going to bed, is Savion sleeping?" Ms. Naomi questioned.

"Yes, but you look tired I can just take him to the hotel with me," Love said to her.

"No, let him stay, we will be alright. I want him to stay with me for a few days," she stated, and Love nodded.

"Is it safe for me to leave now?" Love questioned Sin.

"Yeah, you both are safe now. Tay, are you coming home with me? I really need to get some rest," Sin asked, and I looked over at Love.

"Tay don't worry about me; I will be fine. Everybody has been through a lot in the last couple of days. Go spend some time with your man, I will talk to you tomorrow," Love stated, she gave Sin and I a hug, and turned to leave.

"Love, I'm sure Law is going to want to talk to you soon. Just not tonight. He is really in a bad place right now," Sin spoke.

"Okay, she replied and walked out of the door. Sin walked up to me and pulled me in for a hug. This has been one stressful fucking day, let's get out of here." He kissed me on the lips, and we headed back to his house. By the time we made it back to Sin's place he had filled me in on all of the shit that had taken place. I was still sitting here with my damn mouth wide the fuck open. I felt so fucking bad for Law, and I wanted to beat the shit out of Zion's punk ass. I know that Love was gonna go the hell off. Law daddy was a piece of fucking work, damn! He was sticking dick in every damn body.

"Taymar you know I want you with me all the time," Sin stated, as he crawled in bed with me.

"How can that be when I live in New York, and you live in Philadelphia. I'm not sure that I want to move back here," I told him, and I was being honest.

"I guess we got some shit to figure out then. There is no way in hell I'm sleeping in this bed another night without you," Sin said, and pulled me on top of him kissing my lips. He pulled my tank top over my head, as he leaned up and began gliding his tongue over my nipple and latched on.

"Shit!" I moaned, as he began to lick and suck all over my damn chest. Grazing his fingers over my pearl caused me to prematurely cream. I didn't know what the fuck was different about tonight. But every time he touched me caused me to shiver and my pussy to jump.

"So, you not gonna move in with me, lil' mama?" he asked, as he nibbled on my bottom lip.

"Mmmmm, mmmmm, I can't do it right now. That's something..... Ohhh shit!" I moaned, as he slid his finger inside of me.

"Damn that pussy is wet," he whispered in my ear.

"Mmmmm, shit," I gritted, trying to hold it together, but the shit was just too good.

"Taymar you're not fuckin leaving me and going back to New York. You and this good ass pussy will be right here every damn night in my bed!" he growled, as he slid his dick in me with force!

"Ohhhhh shit! Fuck me daddy," I screamed out, as I began squirting all over the damn place. He continued to dig deeper, and deeper hitting my spot causing me to lose my damn mind.

"Are you moving in with me, Tay?" he questioned, as he pulled out and slammed his dick back in me, damn near taking my breath away.

"Hell yesssss! Ohhhh shit!" I screamed, and he flipped me over to hit it from the back. I was creaming and fucking screaming for hours. This nigga dick game was fucking lethal, I knew I should have prayed to the good dick Gawwds before I fucked his ass. He was sleep, and I tiptoed out of the room to call Love. I needed to talk to her ass, so she was gone have to wake the fuck up.

"Tay it's three in the morning, is everything alright?" she asked.

"Hell nawl! Everything ain't alright! This good dick nigga done got me to agree to move in with him! Bihhhhh can you imagine me getting this type of dick every damn day, cause I can't. This good dick, big dick nigga gonna be done rearranged my muthafuckin uterus and slid that bitch up near my tonsils! Mmmm, mmmmm, hell nawl! We gotta pray, bow yo head bihhhh! Good dick gawd I promise I will never look at a fine, big dick, good dick nigga ever again if you get me out of this good dick situation. I promise to only fuck with ugly, pencil dick niggas for the rest of my days! Let the church say, Amen!" I said, but all Love goofy ass was doing was laughing.

"I thought you said you weren't fucking with him no more. What happened to the clink clink method?" Love asked as she burst out laughing again.

"You know you a silly hoe! The clink clink shit went out

the window as soon as that good dick nigga blew on my ass," I told her.

"Girl, I swear yo ass is crazy as hell. I'm going over to Grammy's house tomorrow, I'm having a contractor come out and fix the damages. Mr. Tommy from down the street boarded the windows but that's not going to last," Love stated.

"Yeah, and we need to clean up that mess," I told her. We agreed to meet at Grammys and get her house back together.

.

Chapter Twelve

SIN

I called to check on Law, but he hasn't been answering his phone. My mom said she went over this morning and he was still in a fucked-up mood. I dialed up Cam to see what the deal was from the warehouse after we left.

"Talk to me," he spoke.

"Bruh, how are we looking?" I asked him.

"It was about five mil in there, it's locked away. But we still have that meeting with the connect this week."

"We will be ready for it, good looking out. I will hit you later, I'm going to be spending some much-needed time with my family," I said to him, and we ended the call. I was dropping Tay off to her grandmother's house to meet up with Love. I think I need to go and check on my brother. I'm worried about him; I pray this doesn't push him over the edge.

"Babe are you ready?" I asked Tay.

"Yep, let's ride," she responded, walking out with them tight ass jeans on. I wanted to take her fine ass back to bed. Taymar was a beautiful girl, and damn did she have me wrapped around her fucking pussy. I had to show her ass who was boss though, even though she got me wrapped the fuck up. I know I had her ass right where I wanted her to be. Fuck that! There was no way that she was taking her ass back to New York. About thirty minutes later we pulled up to Ms. Josephine's house and Love was standing outside talking to the contractors. The workers had already begun replacing the windows and a new door was put on the house. I felt so bad for kicking that damn door in, the neighbor tried his best to fix it, but it surely needed to be replaced. I got out of the car with Tay, I wanted to let them know that I would take care of the bill.

"Hey y'all," Love spoke.

"Hey sis, I see you trying to get the house back in order. Let me know what the cost is, and I will pay for it," I told her.

"We're good, thank you for offering to help, but I got it," she stated, and that shit was not going to happen.

"Nah, I got this, spend that money on my nephew," I smiled, and she finally agreed.

"What's up y'all," Gabe spoke, as he walked up the sidewalk.

"Hey man, what you got going on?" I asked, as we dapped it up.

"Nothing much, Taymar told me she was going to be here. So, I wanted to come and talk to her without the damn bullets flying!" he stated, and I could understand that.

"Gabe, she's in the house, you can go ahead inside," Love told him.

"Nah, I'm good, I will wait on her out here," he responded, looking all around.

"Nigga what's wrong with you, you good?" I asked him, because this nigga had my ass looking around.

"I'm straight," he said, as Love called Tay outside.

"Hey Gabe, why the hell are you standing out there bring yo ass inside. I'm cleaning up this mess in here," Tay told him.

"I will wait until you finish," he said to her.

"Boy we don't have no damn roaches, rats, or no damn raccoons! Ion know who the hell you been around with that shit, but it fucked yo black ass up! Now bring yo ass on in this damn house!" Taymar fussed.

"How you know they ain't in there, you told me y'all been gone for the last couple of days. When we were here yesterday, that damn door was barely up! I'm good, you better watch yo back while you in there. But if you die from them biting yo ass up, I promise to find out if we're brother and sister. I will make sure to send you out in style, what color you like blue, or black? Maybe a burnt orange would look good on you," he said to her, and she was standing there ready to go off on his ass.

"Nigga get the fuck in here if they get my ass, we're going the fuck out together. I knew I should have left your ass where the fuck you was at. The lawd done blessed me with a maybe crazy ass brother!" Taymar yelled, as he ran to his car and grabbed a duffle bag. The two of them together was too damn much. If they were sister and brother that means I had to deal with them both!

"I'm gone come in there, but if something happens to us and they only got one spot in heaven. I'm pushing yo ass down, so I can get the hell in first. Fuck that! There will be no ladies first at the pearly gates on that damn day," Gabe told her, as they went back and forth. Love and I were laughing so damn hard, my damn chest was hurting. This nigga thought they had bugs in the damn house!

"Yo, let me get the fuck out of here. This nigga is crazy, they don't need to take no damn DNA test. They are brother and fucking sister," I said to Love, and she agreed with me.

"How is Law doing?" Love asked me. I knew she was worried about him; she was just going to have to understand how he was feeling and wait this out. The only person that could get through to him was our mom. She was even having a hard time with him, and that had us both worried.

"He is pissed, and not in a good head space right now. I'm actually on my way over there to check on him," I told her.

"Okay, let him know that I asked about him," she responded. I hugged her and hopped in my car, to go see about my brother.

Chapter Thirteen

LOVE

*I*t was going on eight and I had nothing to do, I checked out of the hotel and was now back at my Grammys house. I called and told her the house was fixed and that she could come home if she wanted. Although, she was very happy to hear about her house. She decided to stay with my aunt for a couple more weeks. I was glad that she wanted to stay longer because she needed the time away. Taymar was out with Sin, and Savi was still at Ms. Naomi's house. It was killing me trying to stay away from Law. I really wanted to be there for him, I know he is going through a tough time right now. My phone was going off, I grabbed it before it stopped ringing and I saw that it was Gio calling.

"Hello," I greeted.

"Ahhh, she answers," he stated.

"Gio, I'm so sorry, I know we were supposed to go out.

But I had some family issues going on. Can we do dinner tomorrow night?" I asked him, it had totally slipped my mind that I was supposed to go on a date with him.

"It's all good, baby. Tomorrow night sounds good, are you alright?" he questioned.

"Yes, everything is good now. I will see you tomorrow night," I told him, and we ended the call. Needing to see Law had gotten the best of me, maybe I can get him out of the house and his mind off of all of the drama. I jumped up grabbing my purse and headed out the door. I arrived at his apartment building about twenty minutes later. I called Tay because I was so nervous about seeing him. Maybe I should have listened to what Sin had said, and let Law come to me when he was ready. Tay must have been busy because her voicemail picked up, I hit the call button again.

"Hey, L, what's up?" she questioned.

"Hey, I decided to come and check on Law. I'm worried about him, I couldn't just sit there while he's hurting," I said to her.

"Ahh damn! Girl he gone fuck the shit out of you, like he really gone fuck the shit out of you! The fuck that he is going to put on you, is going to be so damn gangsta! Biiihhhh, yo pussy gonna pay for everybody else fuck-ups and mis muthafuckin haps! Like he gone fuck the shit outta you for Shantel fucking his pappy! He gonna fuck the shit outta you for his pappy being a pus bitch! The one that's gonna really get you fucked the worse, I mean the dick probably gone get stuck in a lung or some shit. Is that you kept his son away from him. He still ain't pay yo ass back for that one yet. Wheeewwww chile, make sure he got some Epsom salt, cause you gone need that shit!" she went on and on.

"Really, Tay!" I laughed.

"Yesss bitch, really! You gone pay for all them niggas tonight. Especially if you take your ass up in there! You want me to call you in like thirty minutes, so I can get you out?" she asked me.

"I will be fine, ohhh yeah, I'm going out with Gio tomorrow night," I told her.

"No, the fuck you not, because you gone have an issue with Law if you do," she laughed.

"Law is not my man, I'm free to see who the hell I want to see," I stated.

"Okay, do you, and see how that shit works out for you," she responded, and we ended the call. I grabbed my purse and walked inside the building.

"Hello, I'm here to see Savion Williams," I said to the security guard.

"What's your name, and I will check to see if you are on the list," he replied.

"My name is Love Hill, but I don't think I'm on the list," I stated.

"Actually, you are on the list, Ms. Hill. Do you need the penthouse number?" he asked.

"No sir, I have it. Thank you so much," I told him and went to get in the elevator. I assumed that he added me to his list because I have his son. When the elevator made it to his penthouse I stepped off. It was dark inside, but I could hear music playing in one of the rooms. I followed the sound and prayed that I wasn't walking into him in bed with another woman. I knocked on the door, but I didn't get an answer. I opened the door and walked into the dimly lit bedroom. He was lying in bed on his back, I called out his name lightly as I stepped to the side of the bed.

"Law," I called out and touched his arm.

"What are you doing here?" he asked, without opening his eyes.

"I wanted to come and check on you, are you alright?" I asked him.

"I'm good, is Savion alright?" he questioned with his eyes still closed.

"Yes, he's with your mother," I told him.

"Why did you let that pussy ass nigga talk you into keeping my son away?" he asked angrily.

"What?! I didn't let him do anything! I made the decision, he just suggested that it was best for Savion. He said that he would help me every step of the way, but ultimately the decision not to tell you was my decision alone. There were times when I felt like you needed to know, and he would get so angry. To the point where he would hit me, and at that time even though I still loved you. I was fighting to keep peace in my marriage, it wasn't until his abusive ways became an almost everyday thing, along with the cheating. He must have gotten tired as well because we both agreed to split," I said to him, not really understanding where all of this was coming from.

"Did you know he was Jax's son, and Tee was his sister?" he questioned, and I was confused as hell.

"What?! Jax is Zion's dad? Zion said he didn't know his real father! I didn't know that, how is this possible? Oh my God, Zion is your brother?" I asked him, I was standing here in total fucking shock. I hope he doesn't think that I was involved in any of Jax's wrongdoings. I would never do that, keeping Savi away was bad enough. But I would've never done no shit like that, I told him the truth regarding why I kept Savi away.

"That nigga is no brother of mine!" he roared.

"I'm sorry, I didn't know about any of that. I did know that Teana was his sister, I just didn't know that Tee was the same person until Sin showed me her picture last night. I can't believe this shit," I stated. Why wouldn't Zion tell me some shit like that? He knew I had slept with Law, and he knew that Savi was Law's son.

"I don't ever want my son around that nigga, ever!" he yelled opening his eyes, and I jumped.

"I understand," I whispered, and turned to walk away. When I made it to his bedroom door, I was being pulled back and pushed against the wall.

"Where are you going?!" he gritted.

"You're in a bad mood, and I don't want you to disrespect me anymore. I guess we can see each other when you feel a little better," I told him, and he crashed his lips into mine.

Hungrily attacking my lips and neck. Every time he kissed or touched a place on my body, I was on fucking fire. He pulled my shirt over my head, and unbutton my jeans sliding them down my legs. The conversation I had with Taymar earlier popped into my head, and I was officially scared as fuck.

I tried the clink clink method with my legs, but when he slid his hand inside my panties and his finger grazed across my pussy. I lost all self-control; a moan escaped my lips just as he slid his tongue inside. Pulling my panties off, he lifted me, and my legs wrapped around him without thought. He began sucking and licking on my breast, giving each of them equal attention. Just the touch of him had my ass cumming and he hadn't even put the dick inside of me yet. He walked with me pressing my back up against the big floor to ceiling window in his bedroom.

"There's nothing that will stop me from entering you tonight," he gritted, as he pushed that monster dick inside of me.

"Ahhhhhhhhhhh, fuck!" I screamed out, as the tears slid down my face. He began thrusting in and out of me, causing my pussy to grip his dick. The feeling was so surreal, I have never in my life felt dick so good. I closed my eyes to try and stop the tears and enjoy this ride of pleasure, that shit didn't work.

"Open your fucking eyes and look at me when I'm inside of you!" he growled, as he gave me death strokes, it felt like he was ripping my ass apart. I didn't give a damn, it felt so fucking good!

"Ohhh my fucking Goddddd! I can't fucking take it!" I cried out, digging my nails into his back.

"Stop calling that nigga, he can't save you tonight! You're going to take everything I have in store for your ass! Do you know how long I've been wanting you, all the years of pain I felt with you not being with me!" he roared, as he slid out of me, placing me on my feet and turning me around to enter me from the back.

"Urghhhhhhhhhhh, fuck this pussy is fucking paradise!" he spoke as he pulled out, then slamming back inside of me.

"Shit, fuck me, Law! Oh, Lawwwwww!" I screamed.

"That's right baby, that's the only name you should be calling!" he gritted and continued to fuck my life all the way up. I came so many times and in so many positions I could barely walk. The next morning, I woke up, and he wasn't in bed. I pulled my phone out and saw that I had twenty-three missed calls from Tay. I had a few voicemails, so I hit the play button.

New Message *Love bitch you alright over there. Don't forget to clink clink hoe!*

Next message *Bihhhh oh my Godddd he fucked you, didn't he?! I told yo ass not to go up in there, yo ass ain't gone never be able to walk again! Call me back!*

Next Message *Good dick gawwwds, I come to you as a humble hoe, asking that you watch over my cousin Love. Please give her pussy and mind the power to get the fuck up and walk like regular people oh Gawd. Give her the power to stay away from the good dick bastard from the good dick academy, gawwwd! I pray all these things in yo name*

Gawwwd, Amen! I was in here crying, I mean I had real fucking tears flowing down my face.

"Is everything alright?" Law asked as he walked out of the bathroom with water dripping from his body. Good lord, this man was beautiful. It has been years since I've seen him in the nude and damn the lord was good to him.

"Ummm yes, I was just listening to a voicemail." I stood to walk in the bathroom, and I could barely move. I heard him chuckle, I decided to just keep walking and not entertain his ass. I would have to take a warm bath later; I turned the shower on and waited for it to warm up. I saw that he had already placed a towel, washcloth, and toothbrush in the bathroom for me. By the time I was done he had made bacon and eggs for me.

"Thank you for this, I'm starving," I said to him.

"No problem, I called and checked on our son. Mom said he was in the back yard playing with her neighbors' son," he stated.

"Ahhh that's nice, he's making friends," I smiled.

"Yeah, that's cool," he said.

"Law, what is this that we're doing? I know that it just happened, but I guess I need to know," I looked over at him.

"We were just two people that needed each other, I'm not ready for anything serious. My heart can't take what you did to me seven years ago," he spoke, and my feelings were hurt. But I had to accept what he was saying.

"Okay, I think I better go, I have some things to take care of," I told him, as I stood to get dressed.

"Okay," he said, and grabbed the dirty dishes and walked out of the room. I couldn't believe that he was acting so disconnected after the night we shared. The tears were burning my eyes, and I refused to let them fall. I moved as fast as I could to put my clothes on, but my body was in so much pain. When I was dressed, I went straight for the door without saying goodbye. I could understand his feelings, after everything that has happened to him. But damn did his rejection have to hurt so bad. When I made it back home, Tay was in the kitchen making a sandwich. I tried my best to sneak past her, but that shit didn't work.

"Mmmm, mmmm! Bring that ass on in here, bitch. Gone head and get yo limp of shame on out, because I know your ass can't walk," she laughed. I did just that. I walked in the kitchen limping because my ass was hurting. If Law did nothing else, he fucked me into next year, it has been years since I had sex and that shit showed last night.

"It was so good, Tay and my heart is so heavy right now," I told her, as the tears fell.

"Ahhh shit, the good dick alliance got you boo, it's going to be alright. We all get got sometimes look at my ass, this nigga got me moving right on in with his ass," she said, and I smiled at her.

"It's not even that, he doesn't want me. It was just two people that needed each other type of fuck," I told her.

"Oh damn, he said that?" Tay asked in surprise.

"Yes, so I'm moving on. If I like how my date turns out tonight, I'm going to give this a try with Gio," I responded.

"I think that you should do whatever is going to make you happy. If I was you, I wouldn't just settle down with one guy. Get back out there and date, you never know, Gio may not be the one for you. My advice is to just be a hoe, hoe's have the most fun any damn way," Tay said laughing, and I joined her. She stood to give me a much-needed hug. I decided to take a nice warm bath and soak, I was going to relax until it was time for my date.

I swear I didn't mean to hurt Love; it was just hard for me to jump into anything right now. I've been stomped on so damn much with the two women I thought really gave a damn about me. Shantel turned out to be the biggest fucking snake! Love hurt me to the core, the love I had for her was just unimaginable. I still love her; I just can't open myself up like that to be crushed in the end. Because the next time won't go the way she thinks it will.

Sliding inside of her last night had my heart beating through my chest, I thought I was having a damn heart attack. The shit between us was just different now, and I don't know if I can trust her again. My mother was cooking dinner tonight, and I wanted to see my lil' guy. I was so fucking pissed I swear if I could bring all these dead bitches back to life, I would murder they ass again. I'm not sure what I wanted to do about this nigga, Zion. Ultimately, he didn't do anything other than be a bitch nigga. It was Love's decision to be with him and it was also her decision to keep my son away. He just fed off of that bullshit, but him putting his hands on her was a different story. I don't give a damn who his dad is, that nigga could never sit down and break bread with me. It was going on eight, and I was supposed to be at my mom's at seven. When I pulled up Sins car was in the driveway. Walking in the house they were already seated at the table conversating and eating.

"What's up, bruh?" Sin asked, dapping me up.

"Dad! You came, I missed you," Savion greeted, running to give me a hug.

"Hey son, I missed you too. Are you having fun with your grandma?" I asked him, rubbing his head.

"Yep, Grandma lets me have ice cream and play games whenever I want. I have a new friend, his name is Jeremy," Savi smiled.

"That's great, son. I'm going to pick you up tomorrow so you can spend some time with your dad," I told him.

"Cool, can we go shopping for my mommy's birthday?" he asked. Damn, I forgot Love's birthday was coming up in a few weeks.

"Yeah, we can pick something up. What's up, Tay," I spoke.

"Hey, I'm glad to see you out," She replied.

"I'm good," I told her, just as mom sat a plate in front of

me. I was starving and needed a good meal. Food hasn't really been at the top of my list in the last few days.

"Tay make sure you take Love a plate home," Mom stated, and it just dawned on me that she was the only one missing. I didn't want that to ever happen, if we were having a gathering, I still wanted her to be involved we did have a son together.

"Why didn't you invite her over?" I asked my mom.

"I did, but she has plans for tonight." She shrugged.

"Plans, what kind of plans?" I questioned, and everybody started looking in other damn directions. Like they didn't hear me ask what fucking plans she had.

"What plans did she have?" I asked again

"How the hell am I supposed to know? She is a grown woman, that has a life outside of us," Mom said.

"She had a date tonight, he's a nice guy too. She wanted steak, so he took her to Capital Grill downtown. But I will be sure to take her a plate, she might work up an appetite later and need to replenish," Taymar smart ass said, and I felt the fire rise from the pit of my stomach. I know damn well Love is not out with another nigga. The thought of that nigga touching her had me ready to murder his ass! I jumped up from the table and walked out of the house. I heard Sin calling my name, but I kept moving to my car.

"Law, runnnnnnn, before that nigga get yo girl!" Tay yelled out, as she burst out laughing. It took me about fifteen minutes to get downtown, I double-parked right in front of the damn restaurant because I didn't plan on being there long.

"Welcome to Capital Grill, how many are in your party?" the server questioned.

"I'm not staying, I'm looking for someone," I stated, as I walked through the restaurant and spotted Love and the nigga from the club sitting near the window. He was holding her hand, and I was about to fucking explode on this nigga. I walked up to the table and lifted her ass right up out of her damn seat and turned to walk out the door.

"What the fuck are you doing, nigga?! Put her the fuck down!" he yelled out.

"Law what are you doing? Put me down! Don't you see that I'm on a date!" Love shouted I didn't give a damn about this nigga or her fucking date.

"I know and the date is the fuck over!" I said to her, as we walked outside, and this pussy ass nigga had the nerve to pull on my damn arm like a bitch. I turned holding Love with one arm and hitting this bitch ass nigga with the other, so damn hard he hit the ground!

"Oh my god!" she screamed.

"Next time get a damn nigga that can protect your ass," I told her, as I placed her in the passenger seat and shut the door. The pussy was screaming and cursing my ass out, I bet his bitch ass didn't move from the spot he was standing in. Pussy ass nigga!

"I can't believe you did that! Why the fuck do you care who I'm with or what the fuck I'm doing. You just wanted the ass and that's it, right? Well, you got it, now take me to my fucking car and leave me the fuck alone! The only thing we both should be worried about is our son," she fussed, and I kept fucking driving. It was a good thing that I only lived about fifteen minutes away.

"I'm not trying to here shit you saying, right now! I was just inside of you not more than twelve hours ago, but yet you're smiling in the next nigga face! Don't fuck with me right now!" I told her, as I pulled into my parking garage.

"Why the fuck are we even here? Take me back to my damn car, Savion! I'm not playing these games with you. I apologized to you about Savi, I told you how I felt about you. If that bitch didn't do you dirty you would be married to her right now, saying fuck me! I was weak last night because I have been dying inside for years just to feel you, and love on you. Wanting to touch you, but deep in your heart, you wanted her! I'm not going to be second best because that bitch, couldn't be your best first!" she yelled, with tears falling from her eyes as she jumped out of the car. I hopped out and grabbed her before she could walk away, I pinned her against the car.

"You so fucking stupid, and I mean that shit with everything in me! You have always been first! How long was I supposed to wait for you to get it right? You dogged me out, it was you that fucked me and left me! Oh, how quick did we forget that shit. Yes! I loved Shantel but she has always played second best to your ass. There isn't a woman on this earth that could take my heart and do what you did to it. Just because a person demonstrates that they desire you, doesn't mean shit if they don't value you! I learned that about seven years ago when you taught me that shit! The feeling I have right now for what Shantel did, is pissed the fuck off, for allowing her snake ass in my life," I said to her. Watching her chest heave in and out from her crying, was pulling my heart-strings.

"I'm sorry, I'm so fucking sorry! I never stopped loving you, I was just so scared, and I was wrong. I made a decision that was really fucked up, you have to forgive me so that we can move on! Please forgive me baby, and let me love you," she cried. Gripping her by the neck pulling her into me, as I crashed my lips onto hers. I damn near tried to suck life back into my body. I didn't give two fucks that we were in this parking garage. Sliding her dress up and lifting her against my car. I slid her panties off as I eased into her walls, we both released a breath that we had been holding for a while.

"Fuck, I love you! I have loved you for so long," I whispered giving her deep long strokes.

"Uhhhhh I love you too baby, shit!" She moaned; I swear I tried to break my dick off in her. The intensity of each stroke had my ass dizzy.

"Damn Love," I hissed, as I leaned down sucking on her neck to muffle my sounds of pleasure.

"Law," she moaned out, and I knew she was about ready to bust by the way her pussy gripped me tighter, and tighter.

"Shit! I'm ready whenever you are this is your show, lil' mama," I gritted. She lifted wrapping her arms around my chest and began riding the shit out of my dick. I heard the sounds of music playing and slowed my pace.

"No, don't fucking stop! I need you, fuck me," Love whimpered, and I gave her exactly what she was looking for.

"Ohhhhhh, God! I'm cumming baby, fuckkk me, shit!" she screamed as she gripped her breast, making the most erotic facial expressions.

"Fuck!" I bit down on my lips trying to keep from screaming out like a bitch, as I released inside of her. I don't know where we go from here, I just know I can't let her go. I'm hoping we can agree to take it slow and work on mending this thing between us back together again. I love her too much to see her with another nigga, that will cause the murder rate to grow rapidly!

Chapter Fifteen

TAY

Two weeks Later

I was on my way to Gabe's house. He called me this morning to come over so that we could open the letter from the DNA test that we took about a week ago. When I pulled up to his house the gates were closed, so I sent him a text message. A few minutes later the gates opened, and I drove in and parked my car. Gabe was standing at the door waiting for me to get out.

"Girl, why the hell are you moving all damn slow? Hurry up before I don't let you in," he smiled.

"If you shut that damn door on me, it's going to be a problem!" I yelled, just as I reached the steps, his ass slams the door in my face. I opened it and walked right on in like I lived there, and this nigga really wasn't going to come back and open the door for me. He was standing in the kitchen talking to this fineeeeee ass man. Good lawwwwd he must have been the president of the good dick academy!

"Boy, you lucky I don't feel like beating your ass! Where is Gia?" I asked.

"She went shopping with the kids, Tay, this is my daddy Truth," Gabe dumb ass said, and I looked from him to this Truth guy.

"Don't pay him any mind, it's nice to meet you, Tay," Truth said, and gave me a hug. Hell, I didn't want to let go, but I knew I had to do it.

"It's nice to meet you as well," I responded, and took a seat.

"So, you believe that this knucklehead is your brother? Are you sure you want that to be a reality?" Truth questioned, and we burst out laughing.

"Tru you got jokes nigga, I'm the best thing to ever happened to yo raggedy king pin ass!" Gabe said to him, and I fell out laughing.

"You two are funny," I told them.

"I asked him to be here because this is my true brother, we were in foster care together and we got out of that shit together," Gabe spoke, as he grabbed the letter and came to stand by me. I was so freaking nervous; my palms were sweating. Gabe decided to read the letter out loud, for Truth and me to hear the results. It was true we were brother and sister; I looked at him as tears filled his eyes. He pulled me in for a hug, and I broke down crying. All these years of my father talking about this man, worrying and wondering if he was his son and if he was alright.

"Every dime I spent was worth it, I feel so relieved! I can't believe I have a brother," I cried, as we continued to hold onto each other.

"When I was younger, I always wondered if someone was ever going to come and get me. Moving from foster home to foster home, as I got older, I made up in my mind that I no longer gave a fuck. I didn't want to see my parents, I felt that if they really gave a fuck about me, they would have come back for me. When I got to my last foster home, I met Truth Baylor and we built a bond, a brotherhood, he was older than me. But he promised me that when he was able to get us out of there he would, and he did. So, in my mind, it no longer mattered to me about my so-called family, that I shared a bloodline with.

"But today lil' sister, it fucking matters, I will always be there for you. You did everything you had to do to find me, and I could never repay you for that. I guess I will get your lil' broke ass out of the debt you got yourself into, trying to find me." He smiled, and I nudged his ass. In the past couple of weeks, we had been spending a lot of time together, getting to know one another. I told him about all the shit I went through and the money I had to spend just to find him. Which caused a lot of other hardships, I never shared it with Sin or Love. I guess I was just too embarrassed, it was just easy to talk to Gabe and now I know why.

"Congratulations to you both, and Taymar a sister of

Gabe's is a sister of mine. Welcome to the family baby sis," Truth stated, and I was in tears once again.

"Now that we got all that emotional shit out the way. You not gone be wearing all these tight clothes for boys to be looking at you. That nigga you got; you need to break up with him because you can't have a boyfriend until you thirty-five," Gabe stated.

"Bruh, you a little too late to be trying to push out orders and shit! My clothes are fine, and the boyfriend stays, besides I already got caught up by the good dick alliance and there is no way out!" I laughed looking over at him because I knew he was going to snap on my ass.

"Oh, there is a way out, it's called Smith & Wesson! I got my nine and my three-eighty, and both my babies love to have a good muthafuckin time!" Gabe fussed, pulling both guns out.

"And what his guns won't do, my forty-five will," Truth added, pulling his gun out.

"Ion want to hear shit bout no damn good dick, and what the hell is a good dick alliance? Don't get that nigga fucked up, you too young to know anything about good fucking dick. Fuck that! I'm about to go buy you one of those chastity belts, and we gone see how much good dick you get after that shit! Fuck wit it," he fussed, and I was the only one in the kitchen laughing. Even Truth was mugging my ass. *Damn, they take this baby sister shit serious!*

"Chill out y'all way to serious, and I'm grown as hell," I told them.

"Not in our eyes, we missed all of your younger years, so in our eyes, you're about seventeen, and we will treat you as such!" he said, and the nigga was serious as hell.

"Nigga you crazy, I'm about to be thirty-one in a few months. Which means I'm grown as hell," I smiled.

"Whatever, you heard what I said. Oh yeah, I made this for you, I got you a pink bag because you're a girl," Gabe stated. handed me a damn bag with raid, a pink torch gun, and a UV light that glows hot pink.

"What the hell is this?" I questioned.

"This kit will save yo life, keep it in the car with you at all times. You got a raid gun for the roaches when they come for you. You will be ready for war because those lil' niggas about that life. You got a torch gun, that will burn any damn thing about a half a mile away. You will need that for shit like mice, snakes, rats, and raccoons. The light is to check these niggas before they come up in yo house and car. You can never be too damn careful; this has saved my life many of days. But don't be a dummy like Truth, he never wants to carry his shit and I always have to save his ass. But I'm done with that shit, he on his own. You better listen to yo big brother, trust me I know what's best for all of us," Gabe said, and I just shook my head and took my damn kit.

"I think we need to take a trip to New York to see dad, do you want to meet him?" I asked him.

"Yeah, I think I do, let's take a ride up there now. I would like to meet him today, I have questions," he said, and Truth agreed to go with us. I decided to call Sin and tell him the news.

"Hey Babe, Is he your brother?" he asked.

"Yes, he is and we both are really excited about it. We are going to New York to see our dad, and I just wanted to let you know. I will be back tomorrow, his brother Truth is going with us as well," I told him.

"That's good to hear baby, I'm happy for you both. You said his brother's name is Truth?" he questioned.

"Yeah, Truth Baylor," I responded.

"Damn! This is a small damn world. Truth Baylor is the new connect that I was supposed to meet up with, but something came up in his camp. They said they would call when they were ready to meet up. This shit is crazy," Sin stated.

"I will mention your name just to see what he says about it. But we are leaving now, and I will see you tomorrow," I said to him, and we ended the call. A few hours later we were walking into my dad's building. Gia called while we were on our way here, and she was so happy for us. We agreed to get together soon and have lunch. This was all so crazy to me; I have brothers to kick it with. Truth was serious when he said he was my brother because that's how he treated me. I used my key to get in my dad's apartment, and his nurse Ms. Diane was walking out of the kitchen.

"Hey Taymar, he's having a rough day today, but I know he will be glad to see you. I see you have company with you," she said looking at the guys.

"Yes, this is Gabriel and Truth. It's good to see you Ms.

Diane did you get the check I sent you?" I questioned her. Since I couldn't get a lot of help from the state, I had to pay a nurse to stay with my dad. Thank God Ms. Diane was able to be there for him because I didn't have anyone else that would do it. My dad's family was so fucked up, he had two sisters and they didn't give a damn about him. They barely came and checked on him, I told my dad that I would never deal with them and their bullshit. If something ever happened to him, I know they better not show the fuck up, because I was going to show the fuck out. I can't stand fake ass people, family or not. My mom's side was almost the same way, there were a few family members that I could deal with but for the most part, it was me, Love, Grammy, and my mom.

"Yes, I got it baby, thank you so much. Your father is in his bedroom," she stated, and we walked to the back. Before I opened the door, Gabe grabbed me by the arm.

"I remember you telling me his first name but what is his last name?" he questioned.

"His name is Charles Grant," I whispered. We walked into the room, and dad was sitting up watching television.

"Dad, how are you?" I asked, and he looked over with a smile.

"Tay-Tay, it's good to see you daughter." He looked over at Gabe and Truth, then back to Gabe.

"Dad, this is Gabriel and Truth, Gabriel wanted to meet you," I told him, and he never broke his stare from Gabe as a single tear fell from his eye.

"I have been praying for you for so many years. The day I

saw your mother in that store and got a good look at you, I knew. Even though she told me that you didn't belong to me, it was just something that nagged me for years. I remember going back to the house she use to live in, and the people next door said the family had moved out. They didn't know where they had moved to, and I didn't really know any of her family. I never saw her again; I don't know if she's dead or alive. I'm so sorry I failed you, I'm so sorry I didn't follow my gut. I hope that one day you will open your heart and forgive me. I'm at peace and if the good Lord takes me today, I'm now alright with that. I don't need to know what you and Taymar found out, because I already know. Just one look at you tells me that you're my son," my daddy said to Gabe, and I swear we all were all in tears. Gabriel didn't respond right away, he just stood there with tear-stained eyes looking at our dad.

"You don't know how good it feels to hear your voice. I often wondered what you looked like, and what you sounded like. I wondered if I looked like you, what characteristic traits of yours, did I have. I have to be honest after a while I gave up on knowing the truth about my family. It may sound crazy, but it helps my healing process to know that you didn't know. You can't help that she lied to you, and I can't blame you for that. But I'm cool if I never met her, I don't want to meet her. If there was an issue, and she couldn't take care of me. She could have been honest with you, maybe back then you would have raised me," Gabe said to him, and just broke down crying.

"In a heartbeat, I would have taken you with no questions

asked. Having my daughter was a blessing, but it just always ate me up inside. Talking to Taymar about it helped me, we just have that type of relationship. We talk about everything, and if you don't mind, I would like to try and have that same relationship with you," my dad told Gabe, he continued to cry, and I rubbed his back trying to calm him.

This was a long time coming, he was letting all of those years wondering out. I'm thought maybe he would want to find his mother. But he said that he didn't and that's the way it will be unless he changes his mind. Today he was able to sit and get to know his father, Truth and I decided to give them that time together. After spending hours with our dad, we decided to hang out and have a few drinks. Truth called some of their friends to meet up with us, and Lawwwd the fine nigga alliance showed up and showed the fuck out! I need to get home to my man before I commit all types of damn sins. They looked so good I had to call Love on FaceTime.

"Hey Tay, where are you? I thought you were stopping by after you left Gabe's house?" she asked.

"He's my brother, and he wanted to meet dad, so we drove to New York for the night. But Bihhhhh that is not why I called you. I need you to stay the fuck focus when I show you this shit. Now as we both know we got some damn fine men at home, well you still trying to figure out if you got a fine man of your own. But if for some reason you don't, you can look at all this deliciousness running around up in here!" I told her and flip the camera around so that she could see my brother's friends. Truth, Meek, Juelz, and Zelan gawwwwd damn!

"Taymar who the hell are you talking too?" Truth asked.

"I'm talking to my cousin, Love," I told him, as I hurried and flipped the camera around. He walked over and looked into the camera smiling at Love, and this bitch started blushing.

"Hey Love, how are you?" He asked, and this hoe giggled like she was in damn high school. He told her it was nice meeting her and walked back over to hang with the guys.

"What the fuck was that, he speaks and yo ass over there giggling like you in damn high school hoe," I said to Love.

"Taymar, who was that? Damn he was beautiful," Love replied.

"That's my brother Truth, and he is sooooooo married! Hell, all of them are, but I just wanted you to see that I was in the middle of a fine nigga Tsunami round this bitch!" I laughed.

"Girl you are so crazy, but we have a lot to talk about so hurry back," she stated.

"I will come by tomorrow," I told her and hung up. For the rest of the night, I hung out with my brother and his friends.

Chapter Sixteen

SIN

*I*t's been a few days since Tay found out that Gabe was her brother, and she has been spending a lot of time over at his house. She hasn't officially moved in with me, we still had to go to New York and get her shit. She was staying at her grandmother's tonight, she wanted to hang out with Love. I got a call from Cam, he said that he was out West, and the nigga Jock was short with my bread. When I pulled up Jock was talking real shit to Cam and Zeno and the way shit been going lately, I'm sick and tired of all that damn jaw jacking. Run my money, or I'm running these muthafuckin bullets.

"Where the fuck is my money?" I asked walking up to this nigga.

"Yo, I don't know why these niggas called you, Sin. I told

them I would have the money for you tomorrow but this pussy ass nigga Cam acts like he can't fuckin hear."

"Nigga I got yo pussy, fuck you and I mean that shit literally, nigga! I got yo pussy in my bed, waiting on me right fucking now! Bitch!" Cam roared, and Jock went for his gun. I sent two to his head killing his ass on the spot. "Get this nigga off the street and get my money to the warehouse. Cam stop fucking these niggas girls, that nigga was about to let you have it!" I laughed.

"That nigga wasn't gone do shit!" he stated as they pulled his body inside the trap until the cleanup crew showed up. I decided to stop by my brothers and see what was up with him. He still wasn't a hundred percent; he was just angry and pissed the fuck off all the time. I thought shit was going good with him and Love. But Taymar told me that it wasn't, I walked in his building and hopped on the elevator.

"Yo, Law!" I yelled as I stepped off the elevator.

"Yeah," he responded walking out of his bedroom. What's up?" I asked him.

"Nothing much, just trying to get my mind right! What's going on with you?" he questioned.

"Just had to rock, Joc's ass he was short on my money and then tried to pull out on Cam's messy ass. Cam was fucking his girl, and had the nerve to tell the nigga," I told him.

"Damn," he replied.

"What's going on with you and Love?" I asked him, just trying to see where his head was at with her.

"Nothing, I love her, I will never stop loving her, but I can't get into another relationship right now," he spoke.

"So, you just gonna let some other nigga have her. If you want her, you need to do what you have to do to get her and keep her. You can't possibly think she's going to sit around and not find her own happiness. She's beautiful, I know niggas are hitting on her ass every chance they get," I said to him.

"There better not be another nigga in her fucking face, and I mean that shit!" he yelled.

"Boy shut yo ass up, you sound selfish as hell!" our mom said, coming off the elevator.

"That girl has been sitting in my damn house every other day crying about your ass! I told her to go out there and get her a man, one that is going to love her! Because you can't get your shit together long enough to love her. You got real genuine love sitting in your face, and you too busy holding onto the past to let your future in! You had a lot of people fuck over you, I get it and she was one of them. I get that shit too, but that girl loves your ass! I can see it all over her, and if you let her go, that's on you," Mom spoke, and walked in the kitchen to put his groceries away. We sat and talked with our mom for a little bit, and then I had to go handle some business. When I finally left Law's crib, I swung by Ms. Josephine's house to see Taymar. I pulled and parked my car, just as Taymar walked out of the house. Some nigga in a Bentley parked in front of their house gets out and she walks up to him. They hugged each other, and the hug was a little too long for my liking. Seeing that shit was enough for me to act the fuck up.

"What the fuck is you doing, nigga?! Touch my girl again, and I'm killing your bitch ass," I shouted.

"Your girl! Pussy get the fuck outta my face," he stated, with a New York accent.

"Sin, it's not what it looks like. There is nothing going on here, he just came to get his keys to get his stuff out of our apartment. This is my roo......" I cut her ass off because I wasn't trying to hear shit she had to say right now.

"Don't say shit to me, fuck your explanation! You out here hugged up with the next nigga acting like a hoe!" I yelled at Tay.

"Hoe! Nigga you need to stop talking before you really fuck up!" she shouted getting in my face, I was beyond pissed I was ready to put a bullet in this nigga.

"Tay let me get out of here before I knock this nigga teeth down his pussy ass throat!" This nigga said, and that was enough for me to beat the shit out of his ass. I would have to say that the nigga had hands, but he was no match for me.

"Sin, Case, y'all stop this shit before the cops come!" Tay yelled, and I could hear Love screaming but I wanted to kill this nigga. I felt myself being pulled off of the nigga, and it was Mr. Tommy telling me to calm down. Instead of Tay checking on me she was over there with that nigga checking on him, and that sent me into another rage.

"You out here checking on this nigga! That's how we the fuck doin it?!" I yelled.

"Shut the fuck up! You out here acting like an ass, just assuming shit calling me a hoe and shit! Fuck you! Don't bring your ass near me, it's the fuck over!" she yelled.

"Whatever let the shit be over then," I roared, walking to my car.

"Sin! Wait a minute," Love called out running behind me.

"Love not right now," I told her.

"Sin what the fuck was that? Case is Tay's roommate from New York, they went to school together. He just got married and had to get the rest of his stuff out of the apartment. He was in Philly, so he stopped by to pick the keys up. You owe her an apology, Tay is not that type of girl," Love stated, and I felt bad. But I was pissed the fuck off, that hug and the way he held her wasn't no damn, we just friends bullshit. Fuck that shit!

Chapter Seventeen

LOVE

It was my birthday, and I didn't even want to celebrate. Shit with me and Law is not what I thought it would be after he came into the restaurant and pulled me out of there. Gio never wants to see me again, he said I had to much shit going on with me. Taymar was going through it, because of the breakup with her and Sin. He has been calling her, but she doesn't want to talk to him. Grammy was still in Virginia, and Savion was with his dad. Tay and I were supposed to go out tonight and celebrate. So, Ms. Naomi was going to get Savi from Law later today. I heard a knock at the door, and I opened it without checking to see who it was. I opened the door and got the shock of my life.

"Zion, what are you doing here?" I asked, and the shit that Law told me about him and Jax came rushing through my mind.

"I had business in Philly, and I remembered today was your birthday. I knew you were still up here, I stopped by the house and your maid told me you were away for a while. I figured the rest out since the love of your life knows about his son," he chuckled.

"We are not doing this shit today. Why are you really here?" I questioned.

"Because I want you back," he stated.

"That's not happening, why didn't you tell me that Jax was your father and Law was your brother? You knew who Law was, the day you met him at my school. Now that I think about it you probably knew who I was," I said to him getting angrier by the minute.

"I didn't know who you were at first, the day I saw him with you I knew exactly who he was. I hated that nigga; he got the chance to be a part of our dads' life every day! All I got was birthdays and holidays, being hidden from his family up here. He loved that lady so much that he never wanted her to know he had another son! How the fuck do you think that made me feel? I told him about you, and I told him what happened between you and Law. I told him you got pregnant, I told him everything! There was no way that I would allow that bitch nigga to take you from me when he had already taken my pops!" Zion yelled.

"Jax was a horrible father to Law, do you think just because he was around Law all the time that he treated him well? News flash he didn't, he hated his son and played his other son against him. He played you against your brother so that he could make Law suffer. All those times that you threatened me and hit me, all because I wanted to tell Law about Savi! It was all due to the hatred you had for your brother. Zion, you need to fix this shit! You didn't do anything bad enough to not have a relationship with him. I'm sure it will take time but he's your brother, what you did to me has nothing to do with your relationship with him. You and I will never be together, you have caused so much damage between us. I could never be your friend again, I didn't deserve half of the shit you did to me," I spoke.

"You think I deserved to watch you love another nigga! Yeah, I cheated on you, you deserved that shit! I was drinking too much and that caused my rage to hit you. You deserved all of that shit, I loved you, and yet you loved him! Fuck that nigga, he will never be my brother!" he roared, as spit flew from his mouth.

"Nigga, you were never my blood! If you touch her, I'm going to kill your bitch ass and your mother will hear of your death on the evening news. Do what's best and walk the fuck away, take that L and move the fuck on. If you have any thoughts of harming her or my son I'm coming for you! Your gangsta is nothing, compared to the hell I will put you through before I murder your ass! This is your last mutha-fuckin warning!" Law roared; I didn't even see him walk in.

"What the hell is going on in here? Ohhhh hell, let me go back and mind all the business that pays me. Law let me know if you need me though, I've been waiting to bust Grammy's shotgun. I wasn't going to use it on you or anything like that,

I will never shoot you. Mmmm, mmmmmm that was never a thought. But I would blow this nigga straight to the chitlin circuit! Just yell out yerrrrrp if you need me," Tay said, and turned to walk back in the room.

"Zion just leave," I told him, and he turned and walked out. I didn't want him hurt, so I pray that he stays away. It's time to move on with our lives, he has a new girlfriend because I saw on Instagram that he was out with her, and shopping for rings. I hope that he does right by her, and maybe he can find happiness with her.

"Are you alright?" Law asked.

"I'm fine, what did you need?" I looked at him waiting for him to answer my question. But he was just staring at me, it was something he always did, and I could never understand why.

"I came to pick up Savi's bag," he stated.

"One second," I told him, as I walked off and Grabbed Savi's bag for him. I walked back to the living room and handed him the bag, and he just turned and left. No happy birthday, nothing he just left. I decided that tonight, I was going to have a good time and move on with my life. I'm done worrying about Savion Williams, I've held onto him for far too long. It was almost time to go, Tay and I went and got our hair and makeup done earlier today. I decided that I wanted to be a little free tonight, so I had on a black mid-thigh body con dress, by Dior. I swear my wide hips, and ass was going to cause problems tonight. I matched up a pair of YSL sandal heels and my YSL clutch bag with my attire. Taymar was dressed in a black bodysuit and she was wearing the hell out of that shit.

"Ahhhhhhh shit, one time for the Birthday girl! You gone fucking kill these niggas tonight boo! Let's go see who son we can snatch the fuck up tonight since we both single," she laughed, as she gyrated her body all around.

"Tay you do know that we're going to Sin's club, right?" I asked her.

"I don't give a fuck, that nigga fucked up, not me! I'm single and free to do what the fuck I want to do," she stated, and we walked out the door. We made it to the club, and it was packed. I decided to valet park.

"Damn I hope we can find us a table," Tay spoke, as we got out the car. I'm so glad the bouncer remembered us and allowed us to walk on in. As we were walking through the club dudes were pulling and tugging on us trying to get our attention. We made our way to the bar, and Tay ordered our drinks.

"Tay, I see a table, I'm going to grab it!" I yelled. *Money-By Cardi B* was blasting through the speakers. Tay was dancing and gyrating to the beat as she walked up to the table with our drinks. She placed the drinks on the table, and she really showed her ass. Niggas were throwing money at her, and I was cheering her the fuck on! It's my damn birthday, so I stood up and joined her. We showed our natural black asses and didn't have a care in the world. *Wet-* by Chris Brown came on and we were fucking this club up, all the attention turned to us. This guy came up to me and started dancing with me, he was fine as hell.

"What's your name?" he asked.

"Love, and yours?" I asked him.

"Marco, I want to get to know you, beautiful. Make sure we link up and exchange numbers before you leave," Marco said.

"Okay, we can do that," I smiled. Just as I turned my head and looked up towards the VIP section, I was looking into the eyes of the man that I have loved for so long. His look wasn't of love and admiration. His looked like he was ready to kill my ass, I still didn't give a fuck. I turned my attention back to Tay and this damn girl was giving a damn show. One of the bouncers walked up to Tay and whispered something in her ear. She nodded her head, as she took a seat beside me.

"What was that all about?" I asked.

"Sin said for us to come upstairs. Fuck that nigga!" Tay spoke, as she sipped on her drink.

"Well don't look now but they're coming our way," I told her.

"This how you're playing it, out here dancing for these niggas!" Sin yelled at her.

"We not together, I can do what the fuck I want to do, and that's fucking with somebody's son tonight!" she yelled, and he looked at her nodding his head.

"Keep fucking with me and see what happens to your ass and that bitch's son," he roared, as they continued to argue.

"So, you were going to party the night away and not come speak to me? You think it's safe to be out here dancing and conversating with that nigga like it's sweet?" Law gritted, in my ear.

"You made your choice, and now I'm making mine," I told him.

"Fuck with me tonight, and I promise you gone have somebody crying over their son in the morning!" he roared and walked the hell off. He sounded like he meant that shit, but I decided that I was going to do me. It was time that I let go and have some fun, it was my damn birthday. I didn't give a damn about his threats and what he had to say. I needed to go to the bathroom, so I told Tay I would be right back. Just as I passed the VIP section, I ran straight into Marco, he pulled me in for a hug and I hugged his fine ass back. I told him that I had to go to use the restroom and I would be back to my table in a few. Before I could put my hand on the handle to go in the restroom, I was being snatched up and pushed against the wall.

"Let that nigga touch you again, and I swear I'm killing him," Law spat, placing his hand around my throat as he kissed my lips.

"Happy Birthday, baby," he whispered into my ear.

"Mmmmm, ummm thank you," I was fucking stuck.

"Meet me at my place when you leave here, we need to talk in more ways than one," he said, as he kissed my lips and walked away. Damn, I know my damn panties were soaked, by the time I was done in the restroom. Tay was all the way turnt, dancing with some dude. We stayed and partied for a couple more hours. We were finally ready to leave, walking outside; I gave the valet my ticket for them to bring my car around. I walked Marco over to his car, and we exchanged numbers. When he pulled me in for a hug, I swear I looked at the door to make sure no one was coming. As soon as I turned to walk away, a gunshot went off and Marco was slumped over. He hadn't even made it inside of his car.

"Ohhhh shit!" Tay yelled out, and I ran up to her. We were both crying, as the bouncer pulled us back inside the club. *What the fuck just happened?*

Chapter Eighteen

LAW

I was on a rampage, I told her what the fuck I would do if that nigga touched her again. I warned her ass, but she didn't take heed and now that nigga is slumped. Sin and I were now back in VIP like everything was good.

"Law and Sin, we need y'all upfront," one of the bouncers said. Sin looked at me with this goofy-ass smile on his face, knowing I was mad as hell. I walked up front, Tay and Love were a complete mess.

"What?" I asked, looking at them both.

"Somebody was shooting, and the guy he got shot!" Love cried.

"Did you know him?" Sin questioned her.

"No, but he was someone I met in the club," she cried.

"Why the fuck are you crying, over a dead nigga you don't know?" I asked her.

"His name was Marco, I walked him to his car and when I turned to leave somebody........." Love stopped talking as if a light bulb went off, and she walked over to me.

"You did that shit, didn't you? How could you shoot him, what the fuck is wrong with you?!" she yelled in my face.

"You need to calm the fuck down; I didn't kill him, you did! I told you not to fuck with me! Blame your pussy not me," I roared, and she went off.

"Fuck you, Law! Fuck you, you don't the fuck own me!" She slapped the shit out of me, and I gripped her up.

"Make that the last time you put your hands on me!" I got in her face and kissed her lips, she rushed out of the club with Tay behind her.

"Really, nigga! You crazy as hell, you really didn't have to shoot that nigga!" Sin stated, and I shrugged. When we walked outside some nigga was bent down in the passenger window talking to Tay, and Sin pulled his gun out and shot the nigga in the leg.

"But I'm the crazy one," I said to him, and he shrugged. The dude yelled out in pain from the shot, as the guards pulled him out the way. Taymar got out of the car going the fuck off, as they went back and forth. I walked around to the driver side and Love was sitting there in tears, just as Tay got back in the car.

"I want you to meet me at my house after you drop Tay off to Sin's house," I said to Love.

"Who going to Sin's?! I'm not going no damn where near that crazy nigga! Fuck him, Love, if you want to fuck with your crazy ass nigga, you can just drop me off to the house! Both of these niggas are the hell crazy," she fussed.

"I'm not going anywhere but home," Love said to her.

"You know I'm not playing with you right now, if you're not at my house in an hour I'm coming to get your ass. Nobody is safe when I'm fucking pissed," I told her.

"Fuck you!" she shouted, and I smiled at her.

"I plan to do just that! See you soon, baby," I told her and walked off. Sin's crew had already removed the dude from the parking lot and the car was gone. I had finally made it home, I decided to jump in the shower while waiting on Love to get here. We needed to really have a serious conversation, watching her tonight pissed me the fuck off. I don't feel bad at all about what I did, I'm not fucking playing with her. By the time I was done in my shower, I heard the shower going in my guest bathroom. I assumed that she had made it and decided to take a shower as well. I walked in the bathroom, and she had just stepped out of the shower. Her eyes were puffy and red, from all of the crying she had done. I guess I kind of felt bad because I probably scared her, other than that I felt nothing. I didn't say anything to her, I just stared at her fine ass. God definitely blessed her.

"Why did you do that? You have been stringing me along, and I'm not waiting on you any longer. You didn't have to kill him," she spoke.

"I warned you, and you didn't listen," I shrugged, as I continued to stare at her.

"You know it's not polite to stare," she stated, as she attempted to put on a tank top.

"Clothes are not necessary tonight," Is all I said, walking out of the bathroom and heading to my bar. I poured myself a drink and poured her a glass of wine. When she walked into the room, I handed her the wine and pulled her in between my legs.

"I'm sorry, if I scared you," I spoke, I knew she was really upset about tonight's events.

"Okay," she whispered.

"Are you alright? Where did you take Tay?" I asked her, wondering if Tay gave in and went to my brothers.

"I will be fine; Tay is still just as pissed as I am. But she did go to Sin's house. She said she would rather tear up his shit, then fuck up some shit at Grammy's house." She responded, sipping on her wine.

"Let's not talk about them, let's talk about us," I told her, taking the glass from her hands and placing it on the bar.

"What are we talking about? I mean I know I'm only here to fuck you, you made it clear that's what you wanted. You also made it clear, that you weren't ready for anything more," she spoke.

"Tell me what you want," I said to her, as I wrapped my arms around her waist pulling her closer to me.

"Don't play with me, Law. You know what I want, I'm just not playing around with you anymore. If you don't want me, I have the right to live my life. I'm here because I want to be here," she whispered.

"I'm not playing with you, baby, tell me what you want," I stated, as I traced my fingers along her jawline and then gripping her neck. Pulling her face close enough for me to latch onto her bottom lip. Her moaning in my mouth, caused my dick to jump but before we went any further, she had to tell me what she wanted.

"What do you want, Love?" I asked as I turned the soundbar on as *Mirror- By Neyo* came through the speakers.

"You! All I ever wanted was you," she responded. I picked her ass up so fast, carrying her over to the lounge couch.

"Law," she whispered.

"I'm right here, baby," I said kissing her lips as she slid her tongue in my mouth. That shit felt amazing, and something came over me that I haven't felt in a long time. The love I had for her was undeniable, and I was tired of fighting to protect my heart. She had that shit, and I didn't want it back it was hers to keep forever. *Say It – By Neyo* came blasting through the speakers and it was the perfect song for what was about to go down in this room tonight.

"I need you." She whimpered, as I kissed, sucked, and licked every bit of her. I ran my tongue over her clit, which caused her back to raise just a little.

"Relax, baby and let me make you cum," I spoke, as I pulled her clit into my mouth. Sucking and licking on that mutherfucka like the world was about to end. Her facial expressions let me know that she was enjoying what I was doing to her. Spreading her legs further apart as I feasted on her pussy.

"Oh baby, please don't stop. Shit!" She moaned out.

"I have no plans on stopping, lil' mama," I gritted.

"Ohhh shit, I'm cumming!" she screamed, and I quickly replaced my tongue with my dick. Entering her with force, hearing her cries begging for more pushed me over the edge.

"Law fuck me! Oh God, fuck the shit out of me. I need all of you tonight!" She screamed. Gripping her thighs, I went beast mode on her pussy. Thrusting deeper, and deeper fucking her G-spot up!

"I can't- I can't take it, ohhhh shit. It's too much baby!" She cried out, placing her hand on my stomach trying to push me off her. I slapped her hands out the way and tried to fuck her senseless.

"Fuck that, you gone take all of this dick tonight! Put your big girl panties on and take this muthafuckin dick! This yo shit, don't you want it, baby!" I gritted, as I bit down on my bottom lip.

"Yessss- ohhh, fuck yes!" she moaned. I was so far gone I didn't even hear her say she was cumming. I just felt the powerful force of her cumming, and her putting a chokehold on my dick as she pulled the cum right up out of my ass.

"Ugggghhhhh fuck! This pussy is so fucking good!" I roared, releasing the most vicious nut I think I ever had.

"Are you alright, baby?" I asked kissing her on her lips.

"Mmmm hmmm, I'm more than alright." She smiled.

"Come on let's go jump in the shower, and then we can

raid the fridge. I'm taking you out for your birthday tomorrow night, so don't make any plans," I told her.

"Okay," she responded. For the rest of the night, I made love to this beautiful woman. For the first time in a long time, my heart felt at ease. We both agreed that we would take it slow, and work on gaining our friendship, and trust back. However, I knew that I wasn't letting her walk out of my life again.

Chapter Nineteen

TAY

I was sleep by the time Sin came home last night and I was locked up in his guest bedroom. I'm glad he decided to leave me alone, I took a shower and walked down the hall to his bedroom to get my clothes. He was still in bed, I assumed he was still sleeping. I walked into the closet and grabbed the bag that I left over here. When I turned around, he was standing there looking like he was ready to pounce on my ass.

"You know I love you, but I'm not going to play games with you. I apologized for overreacting with your roommate and calling you out your name. I'm sorry about that shit, but I'm not sorry about shooting that nigga last night. Be glad I only shot the nigga in the leg, the next time he won't be so lucky. I will do that shit over, and over again until you realize that the only man that's sliding in that pussy is me. I've never wanted something so bad in my life as much as I want you. I want to build with you, have babies with you. I'm crazy about you Tay, I fucking love you girl!" he yelled.

"I need a ride to my grandmother's house," I said to him, ignoring what the hell he just said. I heard him, I just chose to ignore him for now, I was going to forgive him. I just wanted him to beg just a little more, with his tough ass. I turned to walk out of the room, and he was lifting me in the air. I didn't have a lick of clothes on and I knew where this shit was going.

"You not gonna say shit! You were just gone walk away from me," he said as he lifted me up so that my pussy would be in his face. He wasted no time sliding his tongue up and down my folds. The feeling caused me to arch my back, and a low moan escaped my lips. The more he licked the wetter I got, I felt like I was about to cum and he had just gotten started.

"This pussy is going to get a lot of niggas killed, Baby. Damn you wet!" He hissed. He slid a finger inside of me, as I began to gyrate back and forth on it. He applied more pressure as he sucked on my clit, and I was slowly losing my mind.

"Damn your head game is killing me," I mumbled. The more I moaned, the more he sucked, and that shit drove me crazy.

"Give me that cum, baby! I know you want to give it to me," he growled, and it was like the flood gates opened. I was cumming so hard, and he was drinking that shit up. After I got my composure together, I slid down his body, pulling his boxers down. Placing his dick in my hands massaging and caressing it as I slid my tongue around the head. I slid him into my mouth, as I began to deep throat his shit like I was sucking a lollypop.

"Fuckkk ohhh- oh shit! Suck that shit, shorty." He growled, as he held the back of my head pushing me deeper onto his dick.

"You like that baby," I moaned out as his dick began to pulsate, and I knew he was about to cum.

"Ahhhhhh fuck, watch out," he gritted, trying not to cum in my mouth. But I held tight and sucked that cum right out of his ass. He lifted me up and took me back to the bed. I turned around and he entered me from the back tearing my ass up. By the time we finished, it was going on two in the afternoon. Love sent me a text and said that she was on her way to Grammy's house.

"I have to go, I guess I will call you later," I said to him, and he looked at me.

"You guess? Okay, Tay do you but remember what I said. I'm not playing with your lil' fine ass, I want you in my bed tonight," he said, and I walked off to jump in the shower so I could leave. To be honest that nigga had me fucking nervous. An hour later I was walking in Grammy's house, and Love was standing in the kitchen eating a sandwich.

"Hey boo, how was your night?" she asked.

"My night was fine because I was asleep by the time he came home. Bruh, I can't believe Law killed that boy? That nigga was fine too, what a fucking waste! Then Sin goes and shoots Tremaine in the leg!" I said to her.

"I know I'm still upset, but we talked about it. That shit still got me a little nervous though," Love stated.

"Like for real sus, I'm about to call the doctor and ask them to just throw my whole pussy away. If this shit, make niggas act like that ion even want the shit no mo! The nigga got me nervous as hell, I'm driving one of his cars and I noticed that It needed gas. So, I stopped at the gas station near his house and I'm standing at the pump, pumping the gas. When this finneee ass dude pulls up and starts talking to me. Bihhhh you would have thought I was a crackhead looking for my next high. The way I was moving, rubbing all on my neck and shit. Looking around like somebody was after my ass. Fuck that! I don't want no pussy that good! I'm going to the doctor's office and spread my legs and telling his ass to take the pussy out! They can keep that shit," I told her, as I sat there rocking my legs back and forth. While Love, was damn near on the floor laughing at my ass. She could laugh all she wanted; I was serious about that shit!

"Tay the pussy is yours, you can't give it back," she laughed. My phone was going off, and I saw that it was Gabe.

"What's up, bro?" I asked.

"Coolin, what you got going on?" he asked me.

"Nothing much, I may stop by if you gonna be home," I told him.

"Yeah, I will be here," he said. About an hour later I left and went to go hang out with Gabe for a little while. Love said that she was going on a date with Law, and I'm so glad they were working on their situation. I made it to Gabe's and the gate was opened, I got out the car and rang the doorbell waiting for him to open the door.

"Whose car is that?" he asked.

"Oh, that's my boyfriend's car," I replied.

"Oh, I forgot you got a street dude. Ion even know how I feel about that shit," he said.

"Shit, ion even know about that shit either," I responded, and he looked over at me.

"Why?! What that nigga do to you?" he questioned.

"We broke up because he got into it with my roommate which is a guy. He saw me hug him, and he just got out the car spazzing the hell out. He beat my roommate up and said some shit to me that was a little disrespectful, I was pissed and told him to stay the fuck away from me. So, last night Love and I went to his club to celebrate her birthday. Love and I were dancing and what not having a good time, and we met these dudes. When we walked out of the club, Love walked the dude Marco to his car, they hugged and exchanged numbers. Not even a minute later Law shot the dude, and his brains were splattered all over the top of his car. Then as we were leaving the dude that I met, was leaned in the window of the car and Sin shot him in the leg," I told him.

"Damn! My kind of niggas! Law is a bad muthafuckin nigga, I would have never known that shit. That's some cold shit right there," Gabe laughed.

"That shit is not funny!" I fussed

"Yes, the hell it is, that's that unconditional love girl. Sin a cold nigga too, he can be my brother -in law, I like when a nigga cold with their murder game," he responded, as he pulled that long-ass object that was shooting fire, out of his duffle bag.

"What are you doing?" I questioned him.

"I need to clean my torch gun; I have to take care of my baby. If I take care of her, she will take care of me," he said, and was serious about the shit too.

"You are truly crazy, I don't even know how to use no shit like that," I said to him.

"Yo ass better learn, because I'm only going to save you twice. After that you on your own. As a matter of fact, come on, I'm going to teach you how to use it," he said, and we walked out in his back yard.

"This is really nice," I spoke.

"Thanks, we have to walk back towards the woods," he said grabbing a fire extinguisher.

"Why do you have a fire extinguisher?" I asked him.

"Girl so we can put the fire out," he replied, looking at me like I was crazy.

"Now if you ever see some shit that you not too sure of, you just press down on this handle and burn they ass up!" he said, pressing the button and the fire shot out. He immediately used the extinguisher to stop the fire.

"Okay, let me see you do it one more time," I told him, so I can get it right.

"Alright, you hold it like this, and press down and shoot,"

he said, and just as he presses the button. Somebody was yelling his name, we both turned, and it was Gia calling him.

"Ohhhhhh shit! The fucking tree on fire!" I yelled and he tried to put it out with the extinguisher, but the shit wasn't working. The fire was a little too high, for that little ass extinguisher he was holding. This was about to get out of hand and going to be a fucking mess.

"Fuck!" he shouted.

"Ohhh my God! What do we do? Nigga, we don't have no water!" I yelled, the damn fire was blazing on the tree and would soon catch onto the other trees.

"RUN!" he yelled and took off running, leaving my ass behind. I took off running like I was a track star; we rushed in the house and locked the door. Both of our asses were looking out the window like the cops would be here any minute for our asses.

"Gabriel Thomas, I know your black ass didn't just set the damn trees on fire back there!" Gia fussed.

"Gia, that wasn't me, it was Tay, she did that shit! I told her to stop but she wouldn't. Tay don't worry I'm gone put money on your books every week. You will be the only one in jail that's rich, I'mma hold you down, sis," he stated, just as Gia called 911 to get the fire department out here.

"Nigga! Really! I didn't do that shit," I whispered, and his ass was peeping out the window like we were really in trouble.

"Shhhhh you got to prove your love for me and take the rap. Ion want to go on punishment, Gia ain't gone give me no damn pussy for weeks over this shit! She might even try to take my torch gun away. If you take the rap, I will give you whatever you want," he said, and I thought about that shit. I did need a new car because my car was old as hell and on its last leg.

"Whatever I want?" I asked him just to be clear.

"Yep, hurry up she's coming," he urged.

"Deal," and we shook on it.

"The fire department is on the way, they gone fine your ass. I'm throwing the torch gun away, I'm sick of your ass with that shit," Gia fussed at him.

"Gia, my bad I asked him how to use it, and I shot the fire out. I will pay the fine, but please don't take it out on him," I told her.

"Yeah, you know better than that shit!" Gabe fussed at me; this nigga was taking this shit a little too far.

"It's okay, Tay, you just have to be careful with it, I will make sure your brother pays the fine," she said just as we heard the fire engines. Gia told them that we were lighting fireworks and that one of them shot in the trees. They cut them a break and didn't give them any fines.

"Thanks, sis, you're my rider for real!" Gabe said, as we walked back into the house.

"No problem, big bro, and I know just what I want in return," I replied to him.

"What?" He looked, giving me the side-eye.

"I want the new Jaguar SUV special edition fully loaded, boo boo!" I smiled.

"Hell nawl! Fuck that! Giiiaaaaaa I did it! Mmmmm,

mmmmm nope, I the fuck did it! I set the trees on fire! I rather not have pussy then to have a hundred racks gone from my damn bank account!" he fussed, moving fast as hell to go in the house and tell on himself. I was laughing so damn hard, but Gia already knew he had done it. He was getting me that truck, though.

Chapter Twenty

SIN

Two weeks later

Law and I were on our way to meet up with the connect finally. Even though he's not in the game anymore. I only trusted my brother to have my back in case there was a problem. Just because they were cool with my girl and was her family doesn't mean that they were just going to agree to be my suppliers.

"Just keep your cool, and you should be good. He's the connect so he may say some slick shit, just to see how you will react to it," Law spoke.

"I'm good, this shit is important that we get in with these dudes. Tay said she decided not to say anything to him about me, and now that I think about it. I'm glad she didn't say anything, I don't need my girl putting in a word for me, I can speak for myself," I responded, a few minutes later we were pulling into the meeting spot. When we made it to the door, someone opened it up for us. I knew Gabe, and the dude Quad, so the other guy must have been Truth.

"Sin, Law, come have a seat," he said, and we joined them at the table.

"What's up, everybody?" I spoke and took my seat.

"Law, it's good to see you man, it's been a minute," Truth said to Law, and I was looking at my brother like he had three heads. He didn't say one word about knowing this nigga. I guess if he knew his right hands, he had to have known him.

"I know man, how is the family?" Law asked.

"They're good, you know I have a daughter, and son now. I'm trying to talk my wife into giving me another one, but she put the brakes on my ass," Truth responded.

"She needs to, ion even know why you trying to have all them spirits running around you like that," Gabe said, shaking his head.

"Congrats to you both," Law told him.

"Sin, so we know that you're looking for a new supplier. My bricks go for eighteen, and I don't do credit. You pay when we deliver, and you keep our names out of your mouth. We don't like trouble if you run into trouble let us know so that we can step in and dead that shit right away! Quad will be the one that you contact about your product, and Gabe is your contact if you have trouble. Another thing, we don't supply anything less than a mil per reup. I'm not into the nickel and dime bullshit. Are we good on the terms?" he asked.

"We good," I responded.

"Good! I'm glad that shit is over, I need you to go buy your girl a car," Gabe spoke, and we burst into laughter.

"I can do that," I said to him, confused as to why he wanted me to buy Tay a car.

"That's good, I have the exact car right here. It's a Jaguar SUV special edition, they are going for about a hundred G's. She prefers the black with buttercream interior, and light tent on the windows," this nigga said, showing me a picture of a particular truck. I was so damn confused; Truth and Quad were laughing at his ass.

"Sin don't listen to Gabe, he made a deal with baby sis and his ass is going to buy that truck, today! We are actually on our way to pick it up now," Truth said to me, and I was still confused. If Taymar wanted a new car, all she had to do was say the word.

"Damn, my lil' baby got y'all niggas wrapped around her fingers, huh? All she had to do is ask, and I would have gotten her the truck," I told them.

"Nigga! She did ask, just the wrong nigga. I would appreciate that you think ahead and make sure her bank account is stacked, and she has all that she could ever want. Because if yo ass don't do it, then she's coming to my ass! The lil' girl is expensive already and I've only known her for a damn month," Gabe said shaking his head. I guess Tay had this nigga stressed, but I got my woman on whatever she needs and wants.

"She didn't technically just walk up to you and said Gabe

buy me this car. Tell him why you owe her that car, nigga!" Truth stated, and when he told us the story of him and Tay setting the damn trees on fire. We were bent the hell over, laughing at this nigga.

"Nah, I'm good, have fun buying that damn truck! My baby took the rap for your ass and she kept that shit quiet like a rider should," I said to him.

"Man shut yo ass up, that's why I'mma make her break up with yo ass!" Gabe fussed.

"Do what you got to do, but make sure you doing that shit while you're buying that truck," I told him, and we all burst out laughing again.

"Welcome to the team," Truth stood to shake my hand. We all bust it up for a few more minutes, and then we headed out.

"Nigga, you could have told me you knew Truth," I said to my brother, as we pulled in his parking garage.

"It was no need to tell you, you needed to do this shit on your own and you did. Truth is a cool guy, and when he said that they don't do drama, he meant that shit. So, make sure you keep the crew straight, fucking with Baylor can put you on another level," Law stated.

"I got you, what are you getting into today? I asked him.

"I have a beautiful woman, coming over to have dinner with me tonight," he smiled.

"That's what's up, I'm glad you two are working on y'all shit. She's the one for you, stop wasting time and make that shit official," I told him.

"We will see, hit me up if you need me," he stated, and got out the car. I'm happy that he's starting to smile again. When I made it home, Taymar was in the kitchen cooking.

"What's up, beautiful?" I asked, wrapping my arms around her waist, and kissing her on the neck.

"Hey, babe! How did it go?" she questioned.

"Everything worked out, I'm glad that shit is over. Your brother is still crazy, and I heard about your fire-starting ass," I chuckled.

"Babe, that was him, I just wanted to know how to operate my new toy." She smiled. Shit with me and Tay was getting better, we were back on track. We sat down and had a long talk about her life, and mine. We both had a better understanding of what we wanted, and what our goals were. I'm a man about my shit, and I meant what the fuck I said about niggas being in her face. I will never be down with that shit, and as long as we both have an understanding of that, we good. A few hours later, Tay and I were watching a movie when my doorbell sounded off. I opened the door and Gabe was standing there with a frown on his face.

"Tay your brother is here, boy you look like you need a drink," I laughed.

"Shut yo ass up! I wouldn't look like this if we used your bank account instead of mine," he spat.

"Hey bro, why are you standing out there, come in," Tay told him, and he threw the keys to her new truck at her.

"You got it?!" Tay shouted jumping all on Gabe kissing him on his face, and this nigga was frowned the fuck up for real.

"Girl get the hell off of me, you kiss boys and I don't do those type of germs," he said, and she took off outside to check out her new ride.

"You did good, big brother," I said as we watch Tay act a fool over her car.

"Yeah, I guess you better take over from here because her ass is not gonna get a new car out of my ass every year," he responded.

"I got it from here," I said, and I went out to check out her new ride.

"Ayyye, which one y'all taking me home?" Gabe questioned. I offered to take him home, it was the least I could do since he saved me some money.

Chapter Twenty-One

LOVE

*T*wo months later

Things between me and Law was going amazing. We've been spending a lot of time together and I couldn't be happier. Savi was so happy to spend time with both of his parents. My Grammy was back home and was in a better space now that her house was fixed back up.

"Love are you feeling any better?" Grammy asked when she walked into the room with some food.

"No, I don't Grammy, my back is killing me, and I can't hold anything down," I told her.

"I called Tay, and she is coming to take you to get checked out," she said, and I just nodded. A few minutes later, Tay came running in the room.

"Hey, boo," Tay spoke, as she rubbed my forehead.

"Tay, can you....." I jumped up and grabbed the garbage can that was next to the bed so that I could vomit.

"Oh yeah, we have to go and you're burning up," Tay stated.

"Is my mommy, going to be okay?" Savi asked with concern.

"Mommy is going to be just fine, baby," Grammy told him, as she looked over at Tay. About an hour later, we were in the emergency room and they had just called me to the back.

"Ms. Hill, I see that you've been having some back pain, and vomiting," the doctor spoke.

"Yes, it started last night, it hasn't gotten any better," I replied.

"Okay, we will run some test, I do need for you to give us a urine sample and the nurse will take some blood work from you. Nurse Cindy will get you squared away, I will be back in to see you shortly," he stated, and walked out of the room. A few minutes later the nurse walked in and drew some blood, and to get my urine sample.

"Tay make sure you call and check on Grammy and Savi," I said to her, as she sat texting on her phone.

"Okay, I will as soon as we know what's going on. Girl you know Grammy ass is going to want to know what's going on," she spoke. We waited for damn near two hours before the doctor came back into the room to see me.

"Okay, Ms. Hill, Cindy is going to give you something for nausea. I have an explanation as to why you feel the way you do. The blood work and urine sample results show that you're pregnant and that's where the sickness is coming from," he spoke, and I was sitting here with my mouth agape. I have been so caught the fuck up with Law, that we never used protection. How fucking careless of me, and I knew better than to do this shit. We were doing good, but not good enough to throw another baby in the mix. There was still a lot that we had to work on with us, and now we have this to deal with.

"Well, I be damn, you done let the good dick alliance trap yo ass! Doc I need you to go back there and get me some birth control or magic muthafuckin pills! Because I don't want to get none of that shit she got going on! Mmm, mmmm, not the fuck I, I can't deal with having that nigga's babies. He crazy as hell now, imagine if I push out his babies. Fuck that! Better yet, doc do you know how to take out a pussy, cause ion want this lil' clingy heifer no mo. Every time that nigga get next to me, she always jumping and thumping around his ass. The bitch ain't got no loyalty to her owner, so ion even know why she attached to my ass anyway, fuck her!" Taymar went on and on. The damn doctor was sitting here patting her on the back because he felt Tay was in distress.

"Taymar!" I shouted.

"Bitch, wheeettt! I'm just trying to make sure I don't get caught up! You may want to have a crazy nigga baby, I'm just not there yet!" she stated, rocking her legs back and forth.

"We will do an ultrasound, and I can let you know how far you are," he stated and walked out of the room laughing.

"Lovvveee, you want me to call Law?" Tay asked.

"No, I will talk to him about it later," I told her.

"Oh, hell nawl! I'm sure you said that shit the last time you got pregnant, and you didn't tell him until seven years later. Don't you love your life? He gone kill yo ass this time around. Make sure you leave me and Savi everything and I promise to take care of him. Biihhhhh we gone be living it up in Miami! Do you want to be buried next to your mom, or do you want to be buried in Miami? You just let me know and I got you," Tay stated, and I just looked at her.

"Really, Tay! I'm going to tell Law about it," I told her.

"Tell me what?" he questioned standing in the door.

"Ahhhh shit! Father gawwd, I come to you as humble as I know how....." Taymar said, but I cut her off.

"Taymar!" I shouted.

"Huh?" She looked over at me and Law.

"How did you know I was here?" I asked him.

"My brother called me and said Tay had to take you to the emergency room. What's wrong? Why didn't you call me and tell me you were sick?" he questioned, just as I was getting ready to answer him. The doctor and nurse walked into the room with the ultrasound machine.

"Oh, you have another visitor. Is it okay to get started, or do you need a minute?" Dr. Hammond asked.

"Give us a minute, please," I responded, and Taymar walked out with them.

"Love tell me what's going on," Law spoke.

"I came in because I had back pain, fever, and I was

vomiting. I could barely keep any food down, they ran some test and I'm pregnant," I whispered to him, and he just stared at me.

"Say what now? You're having my baby?" he asked, I assumed to make sure he heard me right.

"Yes," I cried, as he walked over and lifted me up into his arms and cradled me.

"Baby, are you sure, are they sure?" he questioned, as tears filled his eyes.

"Yes, they were coming in to see how far along I am. How do you feel about it?" I asked him. If he wasn't happy about it, I could understand because it was way too soon. But there was no way that I would ever think about an abortion. So, I pray that he doesn't say anything like that.

"I'm ready to take you home, and love on you like never before. That's how I feel about it," he whispered, as he leaned in to kiss my lips. He placed me back in the bed and told everyone to come back inside. Taymar's ass was peeping in the door like she had lost her damn mind.

"Tay get your crazy ass in here, girl," Law told her, and she walked in smiling. The doctor did the ultrasound and told me that I was about nine weeks pregnant. He suggested that I find a doctor to see. I guess I had some decisions to make, regarding my home and life that I have in Miami. There was no way that Law was going to be away from the process of having this baby. I know being away from him, is not an option. I was still in shock, but very happy to be sharing this moment with him. He missed out on the moments with Savi, there was no way he was going to allow that to happen again nor did I want it to happen.

Chapter Twenty-Two

LAW

I talked Love into coming back to my place, we stopped by her grandmother's house and picked up our son. I couldn't believe that she was having my baby. Knowing that she's about to give me another child changes so much for me. I love this woman; I always have, it took her coming back for that shit to resurface and slap me in the face. I tried to let go of all of the feelings I had for her when I met Shantel.

I was just a man trying to be faithful to a bitch that was never faithful to me. I wanted to honor my commitment I had made to Shantel, even though I knew I still loved, Love. I knew that it was wrong and that my marriage probably would never work. But I had to try, I guess God showed me that the path I was on was not the path he designed for me. We've been spending a lot of time together in the past couple of months. It was time to sit down and make some decisions.

"L, I love you and I'm clear that I want to be in this with you. Not because we're having our second child, but because I really love you. Hell, I'm in love with you. I don't want to waste any more time, I want you to be my woman, I need you in my life fulltime. I know that you have a life in another state and I'm willing to relocate if that's what I need to do. I have a shop down in Miami and I can work there, I have millions in the bank so if I never work another day in my life, I'm good. Just as long as I'm with my woman and children," I said to her, pulling her on top of me.

"You would do that for me?" she asked.

"In a heartbeat, beautiful," I replied.

"You don't have to do that; I already made the decision that I would move back here. I'm on leave and I know that I can get a job as a Pharmacist anywhere. I was even thinking that I might open my own pharmacy," she spoke.

"That would be dope as hell, let me know and we can get that shit moving. You do know I can't let you go back to your grandmother's, right? If we are making this shit official, I need you with me. All of us under one roof, I know this place is not going to work for us. I was supposed to be looking for a house and sell my other home. I promise we won't be here long, we just have to find the right house and right location," I said to her.

"Okay, I have money so I can help pay for the house," she replied.

"Baby, as long as you live, you will never have to worry about paying for anything over here with Law. It's my responsibility as a man to take care of my family, and trust me when I say I got this," I told her, kissing her lips.

"Are you happy? Have you healed from the shit that you went through with Shantel?" she asked.

"My heart never fully belonged to Shantel, but me being pissed by the deception is still something I'm working through. More so, because she did that shit with a man that I called my father. I knew he was a fucked-up nigga, I just never thought that he would have so much hate in him when it came to his own son. I would never do no shit like that to my son, Savion is my fucking life! He will never feel that type of pain from his father, never," I said to her, feeling myself getting pissed.

"I know, baby, just know that we love you, and I'm here for you. Let's not talk about them anymore. You have your family right here; I will never leave you again. I promise you that I'm here to take this ride with you," Love spoke, and a calming feeling washed over me.

Chapter Twenty-Three

TAY

Things were looking up for me, I was able to get caught up on all of my bills and I now had money in the bank. Thanks to my man and my brother, Gabe has really stepped up as a big brother. He jokes around with me a lot, but I swear we have the best time when we're together. He made a trip to New York a few days ago and he stopped by to check on our dad. He told me last night that he wanted to move dad out of that apartment building he was in. I cried because I have been wanting to do that for so long. The building had no elevators and his apartment was like a little box. Sin even offered to help with whatever we needed, and I was so grateful for them both. We were in New York, moving the rest of my things out of my apartment.

"Babe, are you still going to pick up the food?" I asked him.

"Yeah, I'm about to head out now," Sin replied, walking in the bedroom. I was packing all of my clothes; I was leaving the furniture in the apartment. I spoke to my landlord and he was more than happy for me to leave it.

"I will be back soon, we can eat and then load the truck up," Sin spoke.

"Okay," I responded, as I continued to pack my clothes. About ten minutes later I heard the front door close and I jumped up.

"Babe, that was quick," I said walking into the living room. I was shocked to see who was standing there, and I knew if Sin came back it would be some shit.

"Case, what are you doing here? I thought you got all of your things out already," I said to him.

"I did, I was passing through and I saw the lights on in the apartment. So, you really going to move in with this nigga?" he questioned, and the way he looked at me was weird as hell.

"Ummm yeah, that's my man and that's what I've decided to do. Why is there a problem with that?" I asked him, not liking the tone he was using with me.

"What the fuck, Tay?! You know how I feel about you!" he shouted, and I was getting nervous.

"I know that you're a married man, and you shouldn't feel no type away about me," I tried to walk off, but he grabbed me and pushed me into the wall.

"I love you, and I always have! I married her because you wouldn't give me the time of day. You knew I wanted you because I told your ass! Yet you go to Philly and give this nigga pussy that should have been mine." He gritted, as he applied pressure around my throat, crashing his lips into mine. I bit down on his lip so hard to cause pain, and he slapped me. I felt my nose leaking, and I knew that it was bleeding. I lost my mind and started fighting him off of me, but he tugged at my clothes trying to rip them off. There was no way that this nigga, that was supposed to be my friend with is going was trying to rape me. I continued to fight, he hit me with force again and the next thing I knew, Sin was pulling this nigga off of me.

"Pussy you put your hands on my girl!" Sin roared, as he punched Case over and over again. Beating his fucking ass, but that nigga was about to try and rape me. Fuck that! I started helping Sin beat his ass. He was on the ground, and his face was fucked up.

"This nigga gotta die!" Sin yelled out, pulling his gun out.

"Babyy, wait! We can't do it here, it's too many people!" I told him, as the tears were flowing.

"Tay the way I feel right now, I don't give a damn! I will do the fucking time, fuck that shit!" He roared; I was scared shitless because Sin was unraveling.

"Let me call, Gabe! Baby please just let me call my brother," I told him, as I ran to grab my phone. Case was lying on the floor, still trying to talk shit! I dialed my brother hoping he would answer.

"Yeah," he answered.

"Gabe, I need your help!" I yelled into the phone.

"Ion got no money, I gave it all to charity right before you called," he said, and I didn't have time to play with him.

"Gabe, my roommate tried to rape me, and Sin is on a rampage. He beat him pretty badly and......" he cut me off.

"Stop talking, send me the address and I will send someone to you. I'm on my way, but you know it will take me a couple of hours to get there. Put me on speaker and let me talk to Sin," he requested.

"Okay, you're on speaker," I told him.

"Bruh, I'm sending someone to you. I'm on my way but put that situation on ice until I get there!" he said to Sin.

"Hurry up, because I don't know how long I can wait! This bitch gotta go!" Sin angrily spat and Gabe hung up.

"Tay are you alright?" He walked up to me because I was truly a mess. I never had to endure no shit like that. I don't give a damn how long, I've known a person. That was truly fucked up! If Sin hadn't walked in, God knows what might have happened. This little bruises to the face, I will heal from. I don't think I would have healed from no shit like rape though. For that alone, I agree with my man his bitch ass has to die! Fuck that! About thirty minutes later, we heard a knock at the door and Sin opened it. It was my brother's friends that we hung out with.

"What's up, Gabe called and said you had a problem. I'm Zelan, and this is Meek," he said to Sin.

"Taymar, are you alright baby girl?" Zelan asked, and I shook my head no. Sin told them what happened, and who Case was. Case was on the floor, barely hanging on but he managed to plead for his life. Zelan kicked him in the face, and that knocked his ass out. A few minutes later, another knock came to the door. Meek opened it, and some guys walked inside.

"They will transport him to one of our facilities, Gabe said he wanted him alive!" Meek spoke, and Sin was still going off.

"Thanks, man, I appreciate it! This pussy was really getting ready to try and harm my girl," Sin told to them.

"I know how you feel, I've been in your shoes before. Shit like this fucking burns me the fuck up, no man or woman for that matter, has the right to violate someone in that manner. Where I come from, we are the judge and the muthafuckin jury. She's family, and I was told that you just joined our team. So, that makes you family, trust me when I say this, we make problems go away," Zelan spoke. I'm so grateful that my brother and his friends were there to help us. I was fucking mad as hell, how could Case even think this shit was cool? I knew how he felt, he told me that shit when we were in college. We talked about it, and I told him what it was, I thought he understood because we never talked about it again.

Chapter Twenty-Four

SIN

I can't even get my mind right I'm so fucking pissed! But I knew some shit was not right when I saw that nigga hugged up on my girl. When I heard her screaming and saw that nigga on her I lost my mind. I was ready to kill that nigga right then! I didn't give a fuck about jail; I would have done my time proudly! Fuck that shit, but Tay calmed me down enough for us to think that shit through. We had made it to the warehouse where they took his bitch ass, and he was now awake. Screaming for us to let him go, nahhh pussy you won't be walking up out of here alive! Gabe had called and said he was about twenty minutes away. I tried to take Tay to get her face checked out, but she said she would be fine and didn't want to go. She was clearly upset, and I had to take a minute and make sure she was really cool. I never wanted to see her hurt, that shit was killing me.

"Taymar! You alright?" Gabe came walking through the door with Truth following behind him. Their faces matched mine, full of fucking anger.

"I'm fine," she cried in his arms, and that shit fucked me up.

"Look what this bitch did to your fucking face!" Gabe roared, as he pulled his gun and sent a shot into that niggas stomach. Case screamed out from the pain, as I pulled my shit out and sent a shot to his arm.

"Ohhhh shit, is that the type of party we're having in here tonight!" Meek smiled, as he sent a shot into his body as Truth, and Zelan followed.

"Bruh, this your woman you can do whatever it is you need to do to this pussy ass nigga! I won't take that away from you, but I had to make his ass feel something from me," Gabe said to me. When I stood up to off this bitch, Tay grabbed my arm.

"Let me do it, he tried to hurt me," she said. If that's what she wanted, then I was damn sure going to let her do her thing. I passed my gun to her, and she pushed it away letting me know she didn't want it.

"Bro, did you bring your bag?" she asked Gabe.

"Never leave home without it, but I see yo ass did! See I knew you had some Truth tendencies floating around in your ass. You gone give me a hard time, just like his ass does. Urggghhhhhh! What you want out of my bag?" He asked her after he finished fussing.

"The fire," she said, and Gabe started smiling.

"I got you, baby sis! Set his bitch ass on fire! This is going to be a damn movie, let me get my damn cheese puffs and beer too. Gabe handed Tay the fire torch, they had Case hanging from a chain as he begged Taymar not to kill him. She spit at him and presses the button on the torch sending the fire straight to his dick!

"Ohhhhhh shit! Baby sis, you haven't been fucking with GBC have you? Because ion want you hanging around them if they contact you just hang up. They not setup like normal people, once you get pulled in your life will never be the same," Gabe spoke.

"Nigga, shut yo ass up! You were on the phone with Ma Lai, on the way up here," Truth said to him, and Zelan shook his head. I was still trying to figure out who the fuck was GBC.

"Did you tell her what happened?" Zelan asked Gabe.

"Maybe," he shrugged.

"This is going to be a long damn night, you know how her ass is," Zelan fussed. Tay ignored them and shot more fire on Case, and that nigga was in flames. He let out a deadly scream, and then his screams went silent.

"Brother I'm really liking this gun," Tay told Gabe and all of sudden we heard the door to the warehouse open.

"Where he at?! Who wants this muthafuckin smoke?!" this lady shouted walking into the warehouse, with another lady behind her.

"What the hell is that on yo.... Is that a muthafuckin

monkey?! Wait is that nigga smoking a blunt?!" Gabe shouted as he snatched his torch gun from Tay.

"Ma, what the fuck are y'all doing here?" Zelan asked her.

"Gabe called, and so here we the fuck go! He told me his sister was in trouble, so we came to bring that muthafuckin heat! But damn, I see that nigga got enough heat already!" She laughed.

"Damn, we missed all the fun," the other lady spoke, as she pulled a blunt out and lit it. Tay and I were looking at each other confused as hell. We knew that the ladies were related to Zelan and they came in here ready for war.

"Ma whatever that lil' bitch is on yo damn neck, he needs to stay his ass over there. I swear if it comes near me, I'm blowing that lil' muthafucka up! You always come with some type of damn animal and shit. See Tay this is why you don't need to hang with these type niggas. They deadly as hell, and they not good role models!" Gabe said, and everyone burst into laughter.

"Sin, and Tay this is the Queen of the family Ma Lai, and this is our aunt Cynt. They about that life, and love to step in when the family is in trouble," Zelan said.

"It's nice to meet you both," Tay greeted them.

"You gonna wish you didn't say that shit, cause them niggas ain't nice at all! I bet you that lil' monkey got a gun behind his back. That lil' ugly bastard got something fucked up that he can do. Because she don't have no regular animals on her damn team, them niggas are deadly just like her ass. I bet you all the money I got, that's a lil' gangsta ass monkey," Gabe responded, and Ms. Lai was bent over in laughter.

"She do have tricks, nigga! That's why I call her Trixxy, bet you won't fuck with her," Ms. Lai told him.

"I bet she better not come over here, or her Trixxy looking ass gone be burntsy fucking with me!" He fussed. This group of people was indeed funny as hell, but Tay wasn't in the mood to have any fun.

"I appreciate y'all for stepping in and helping us out. I think I need to get her home, so she can get some rest," I told them.

"Taymar, I'm glad you are alright, baby girl, if you need anything don't ever hesitate to call me," Truth told her.

"Tay, I will check up on you in a few days. Truth and I are going to hang out up here for a couple of days and I will come to see you when I get back. I plan to go see dad tomorrow and check up on him," Gabe said to her, pulling her into his arms for a hug.

"Okay, I love you, thank you for being here for me," she told him. Tay went and hugged everybody, and she even talked to Ms. Lai for a little bit. I don't know what Ms. Lai said to her but she was laughing which was a good thing. We said our goodbyes and headed back to Philly. Zelan said that he would send someone back to her apartment and have it cleaned out. Tay decided that she no longer wanted anything from the apartment, she just wanted to move on with her life.

Chapter Twenty-Five

LOVE

hree months later

Everything in my life was absolutely amazing, I was more in love with Law than I could have ever imagined, that man had my heart. We moved into our new home about a week ago, and we were adjusting well in our new space. We were about ten minutes away from Sin, and Tay's house. Both Tay and I were excited about that, and Savi loved having his dad with him fulltime. I was five months pregnant, and everyday Law took a picture of my baby bump. There wasn't a day that went by that he didn't kiss on my stomach and talked to his son. I couldn't believe that we were having another boy, I was hoping for a little girl. Law and Savi were super excited about it.

"Hey beautiful, how are you feeling?" Law asked as he walked into our bedroom.

"I'm good, are you going to the shop today?" I asked him.

"Yeah, I have a few appointments, I will be home for dinner. Are you still going to your grandmother's house?" he questioned.

"Yes, I'm dropping Savi off to your mother, and then I'm going to meet Tay at Grammy's," I responded.

"Okay, tell my mom that Savi is our son, and he doesn't live with her. That boy is never home, and loves being with his grandmother." He laughed, shaking his head.

"You call Naomi and tell her that. Do you know how bad she would go off on you, about that boy," I laughed, because he was right Naomi was always calling for Savi to come over, or Savi was always trying to get over to her house. It's because she lets him do what he wants to do.

"Nah, you right it wouldn't go well, I will check on you in a couple of hours. I love you, baby." He smiled, kissing me on the lips and walking out. A few hours had past and I was just dropping Savi off to Ms. Naomi's house. She has been in good spirits lately because she had a new boo in her life. Sean was a very nice man, and she was really feeling him. I was happy for her, and her sons liked him so that was a plus.

"Grammy," I called out.

"Hey baby, we're in the kitchen," she replied. I walked into the kitchen, and Tay was stuffing her mouth. I'm so glad that she was doing better, I can't believe that shit went down with Case. Tay didn't want my aunt or Grammy to know about it, because that would raise questions. He deserved what the fuck he got, my whole outlook on the guys being a part of the streets have changed. I just hate that I made an irrational decision back then that kept me away from the love of my life.

"Hey boo, look at you, you're glowing," Tay smiled.

"Girl, this baby is kicking my butt. Being pregnant is a beautiful experience, but I just want him to come on out," I told her.

"Love, are you ready for Vegas? I can't wait for this vacay," Tay said, and she was right. I think we all needed some down-time, but Law was going out there to work. The tattoo convention was coming up, and we were tagging along.

"Yesss, I'm ready to just lay up, shop, and eat," I responded.

"I just want to tell you girls, that I'm so proud of you both. Love, I always knew that you and Law would find your way back to each other. It was hard on that boy to go all those years loving you. The times that I did see him, you could just look at him and tell that something was off with him. He loved you, there were times that I would be sitting on the porch and I would see his car ride by. He was looking for you, and I've always known that you loved him. Sometimes we make mistakes in life, I'm just happy that it wasn't too late for the both of you to figure it out," My Grammy said.

"I know, Grammy I'm the happiest I've been in a long time. He completes me, and can't wait to see where life takes us," I told her.

"That's good to hear, baby. Taymar, you let Sin love on you, that boy stops by here the other day to drop off my monthly money for my bills. I can't thank him and Law enough for what they do for me," she said to Tay.

"I will Grammy, we're doing good and I truly love him," Tay smiled.

"I need y'all to run down to the corner store for me, I need some sugar," Grammy stated, Tay and I got up and walked down to the store. Walking in the store I grabbed the sugar, while Tay was talking to Lola my grandmother's neighbor. On our way back to the house something felt strange. Like someone was watching us, but when I looked around, I didn't see anyone.

"What's wrong with you?" Tay questioned.

"Nothing, I just feel like we're being watched," I told her.

"Ahhhh hell, I know these niggas don't got nobody watching our ass! Dis tew mucchhh! I swear I'm going back to dating regular niggas. We should have gone for the lil' corner boy that's just starting out! Noooooooo, we want to go after the nigga at the top. I'm telling you now, my next nigga, y'all gonna be embarrassed for me. We don't always have to have the rich thug, with money and a big dick! I want the ugly nigga, with a lil' dick, and ugly friends. If he got ugly friends, I won't be tempted to fuck his friends. Because the nigga would be just as ugly, like the one I got," she said, and I had to stop walking because I was laughing so hard.

"Tay why do you have to be so over the damn top, all the time! You know damn well you not leaving Sin, and if you did you wouldn't be caught with no ugly dude," I told her still laughing at her ass. I had to get something out of my car, Tay went on in the house to give Grammy her things from the store.

"So, you went and got pregnant by that nigga?" the voice said from behind me, and I jumped.

"Zion, what the fuck! Why are you here?" I nervously asked because he looked off.

"I'm in town checking on my dad, and sister. I haven't heard from them in a couple of months. So, I decided to stop by and check on your hoe ass and now I see this! You really fucking that nigga!" he shouted, and I looked to see if anyone was around.

"It's none of your concern, who I'm pregnant by. We're not together, and I'm feeling really uncomfortable right now.

"Shut the fuck up!" He gritted, slapping me in the face as he held a gun to my head.

"Zion don't do this, I'm pregnant," I cried.

"You think I give a fuck about you being pregnant! I don't give a fuck about that nigga, or his fucking kids. You're giving him kids that should have been mine, I loved you and took care of you!" he spat.

"Nigga if you don't let her go, I'm going to splatter your ass all over this North Philly fucking pavement!" Taymar yelled, from behind holding Grammy's shotgun.

"Tay, what do we do?" I nervously asked her.

"Take his gun, and if you make one move, bitch. I'm going to kill you, I put that on everything I love," she spoke, and I slowly took his gun and pointed it at him.

"You two bitches, not going to do shit but let me walk

away. After all, I've done for you, this is how you treat me?! If I get out of this, I'm going to kill you, and your nigga!" He roared.

"No, this pussy didn't! Get your ass in the backseat, now nigga!" Tay shouted.

"Love roll the back windows down. I want you to get out of the car and hold the gun on him while I tie his hands. If that bitch moves, I want you to paint the inside of your car crimson red," Tay spoke, as she took the scarf she was wearing and tied his arms together.

"Tay, we have to do something, somebody is bound to come walking by here soon," I told her.

"Law should be here soon, I called him as soon as I saw that it was this nigga doing all the yelling. Then I went I grabbed Grammy's gun! Fuck this nigga, and then he put his hands on you! Whatever they do to his ass he deserves, you one dumb ass nigga. Law left you alone, but your dumb ass want to come back and be stupid. Now you gone be with the rest of your family!" Tay said, and Zion snapped.

"I knew something was wrong with my dad! I fucking hate you bitch!" he spat, and Tay hit him upside the head with the butt of the shotgun. A few minutes later a car sped down the street, and Sin jumped out of the car. When he saw Zion in the back seat, he opened the door and punch the shit out of him.

"Pussy ass nigga!" he roared.

"You good, sis?" Sin asked me.

"Yes, where is Law?" I asked him, as the tears continued to

fall. Just as I asked that question Law pulled up and jumped out.

"Baby, you alright?" he asked as he looked at my face. I'm sure I had a bruise because he did slap me kind of hard, other than that I was okay.

"I'm fine, he gripped me up and slapped me. He was pissed because I'm pregnant by you," I responded.

"Take my car and go home, everything is going to be alright," he responded, kissing me on the lips. Law and Sin jumped in my car and drove off with Zion in the back seat.

"Tay, does Grammy know what's going on?" I asked her.

"No, she was on the phone when I went inside. I put the bag on the table and came back to check on you. That's when I saw the guy at your car, I didn't know it was Zion until I heard his ass yelling. I ran and got the gun, and called Law," she explained.

"That's good, she doesn't need to know," I told her.

"No, she doesn't, now I got to sneak her shit back inside. Do you want me to follow you home?" she asked.

"No, I will be fine," I said, after hugging her, I got in the car and drove off. I cried because he could have really hurt me and my baby. I knew what was going to happen to Zion, and at this point, I didn't care anymore. All he had to do was leave me alone and go live his life.

Chapter Twenty-Six

LAW

I told this bitch, to stay the fuck away from my woman! Now his ass was going to die, all because he was a fuck nigga that couldn't let go. We were on our way to Sin's trap he had set up for shit like this.

"You can't kill me, I'm your fucking brother!" this pussy yelled.

"Bitch you were never my brother! My brother is the nigga with the gun, you could never be him. You let a fucked-up nigga like Jax influence you to do fucked up shit. The funny thing is, just as long as you had stayed the fuck away from us. I was going to let your bitch ass live!" I spat, as I pulled up to the warehouse.

Sin yanked his ass out of the backseat, and I beat the dog shit out of this nigga. Pulling him from the ground, I drug his ass inside and threw him to the floor. He continued to yell and scream about Love.

"She was my woman! She never loved you and she never will. She married me, that's my muthafuckin son, you were never good enough to raise him, nigga! That's the reason why she kept him from you!" he yelled. Fuck torturing this pussy, I needed him dead. I pulled out my gun and emptied my clip in his bitch ass. I didn't have time for all that talking, his pussy ass knew exactly why he was going to die! Fuck that nigga, I needed to get home and check on my woman.

"Damn nigga, you wasn't playing no games with his ass," Sin spoke.

"I want his as in the inferno," I told them.

"We got you," Zeno responded, and Sin and I walked out.

"Do you think we will ever have peace, the last few months have been hell," Sin stated.

"Let's pray that this is the end of it, and we can actually settle down and enjoy our lives. I'm about to have my second child, and I have the greatest love with my beautiful woman," I told him, I was still fucking pissed about that nigga touching her. I'm just happy that all the bad seeds are dead. I would do that shit all over again, just to be in this moment with her. I dropped Sin off at home and was finally pulling in my driveway. Making my way upstairs, Love was in the bed watching television.

"Let me take a shower, and I will be right back," I spoke.

"Okay," she responded. Love always tries to see the good in people, and even when they do her wrong, she still gives them the benefit of doubt. If a nigga is coming for me and my family, it's my job to eliminate the problem. I was blinded by the shit that Shantel and my pops were doing, and it cost me. When I opened the bathroom door, she was standing there waiting for me.

"I love you," she spoke, wrapping her arms around my neck. Seeing that bruise on her face, had my ass heated.

"You're so fucking beautiful," I whispered, as she pulled on the towel, I had wrapped around me and it dropped to the floor. She kneeled down in front of me, taking my dick in her hands and massaging it. She began licking the head, as she slowly wrapped lips around my dick. She applied pressure as she began, deep throating it had my ass ready to burst. Slowly she started sucking and licking my dick and the shit felt good as fuck!

"Sssssss, fuck! Suck that shit, baby!" I groaned, as my toes dug into the carpet. The moans that escaped her mouth, as she continued to suck my dick. Had me on edge, I felt my release building up from the pit of my stomach and I knew that shit was going to be powerful.

"Ohhh shit," I growled, as my dick throbbed, and the cum shot out into her mouth. I walked her to the bed, and I sat down, with her being pregnant our positions were limited. I rubbed my fingers between her slit, and her pussy was leaking.

"Damn you wet, lil' mama," I spoke. She crawled on me and eased down on my dick, and we both groaned from the feeling. Gripping her waist, I guided her up and down my shit.

The way her pussy was gripping my dick, I knew I was about to tear her ass up.

"Ohhh shit, Law! It feels so fucking good," she cried out.

"This shit is only for you, fuckkkkk!" I groaned and started fucking the shit out of her.

"Damn this pussy..... Oh shittt!" I growled as she started bouncing up and down on my pole.

"I'm cumming! Ohhh fuck, I'm cumming, you feel so good sssssshhhhhit!" she screamed as we released together. I loved the hell out of this woman, and I would do anything to keep her safe and happy.

Chapter Twenty-Seven

TAY

a week had passed, and we were on our way to Vegas. Sin and Law rented a private jet so that we could be comfortable for the four-hour flight. I was so damn excited; it has been a while since I've been on a vacation.

"Law, I'm getting my tattoo tomorrow make sure you save me a spot on your busy schedule," I said to him.

"I got you, but you could've gotten a tattoo anytime. You don't need an appointment, Sin damn sure don't make them. This rude nigga just comes into my shop and sits on my table. His rude ass doesn't care if, I have any appointments or not." We all laughed because it sounded just like my man.

"It's going to be fun watching you do what you love, I can't wait, even though you got us working," Love pouted.

"Yeah, that shit is not cool, we came to relax not work for your ass," I laughed.

"Damn right y'all have to work off this debt, this shit ain't free." He smiled.

"Nigga, I ain't working! I'm going to put that lil' Ink Drip shirt on, but I'm not doing shit," Sin responded, and we believed him. For the rest of the flight, we joked around and had a couple of drinks. Love was mad as hell that she couldn't drink. We promised her that we would drink enough for her, while on this trip. We got settled into the MGM Grand and freshened up so that we could go down and get on these tables.

"Babe, can I play my own hands instead of watching you play?" I asked Sin.

"Lil' baby, you can do what the hell you want to do." He handed me a small duffle bag, and it was filled with cash.

"Ahhh hell, all of this is mine?" I asked getting excited.

"Every dime, you can blow it or save it. It doesn't really matter to me, and this is yours," he stated, handing me a credit card with my name on it.

"Thank you, babe!" I yelled, hugging him and kissing his lips.

"We good, I'm going to always make sure you straight. I can't be making moves out here and you got to ask family to help you out. Nah, shit doesn't work like that with me," he spoke, and I loved him for saying that.

"I think that I'm going to open up a marketing firm. I have a degree in marketing, and I'm good at it," I told him.

"I'm with whatever you decide to do. Just let me know

when you need the bread to get this going," he replied, kissing me on the lips.

"Okay," I smiled at him, I couldn't believe that he would do this for me, but I was grateful. I was having the best time; Love and I won some money and we were ready to damn shop. It was kind of late and we had to get up early for the convention, so we called it a night. The next day we were down in the grand ballroom where the convention was being held. Law and his team were killing it, this dude was good at what he did. I mean people were standing in lines trying to either meet him or get a tattoo. He was so busy I decided to wait until we got back home to get my tattoo done. Shit, he barely had time to eat, Love had to make him take a break. By the time it was over we were tired as hell and wanted to unwind. We all decided to hang out in Law, and Loves suite to eat dinner, and have some drinks. I started pouring shots, and the three of us were downing them left and right.

"I'm fucked up, and all I want to do is slide up in my woman," Law said, kissing all on Love.

"Nigga you always trying to slide up in her ass, that's why she looks like that now," I laughed. I knew Sin was fucked up because the nigga was damn near hanging off of the couch. Hell, I was just as fucked up as they were, Love was the only sober one in the room. Law was so damn drunk he kept staring at Love like he wanted to eat her ass alive. I love the fact that his love for her was so damn raw and real.

"L, I love you so much, baby," he spoke, and Love looked over at him.

"I love you too." She smiled, and he stood up and pulled her up from her chair.

"Let's go get married, I want to marry you right now," Law told her, and I was jumping up and down.

"Yesssss, let's go get married!" I yelled out.

"What? You want to marry me now?" Love questioned him.

"Right fucking now! I'm in love with you, you were meant for me and I don't want to waste any more time. I need you as my wife, I can't go another day without making that shit happen," Law responded.

"Law you're drunk, baby. I don't want you to wake up and realize that you made a mistake. Besides we don't have any rings," she said to him.

"My mistake was that I should have come to Miami when I heard you married that nigga and got your ass. I loved you then, and I love you now! There are several jewelry stores, that we can get rings from tonight," he told her.

"Hell yeah, let's all get married!" Sin drunk ass shouted, and I was clapping and dancing around the room.

"Yes! We going to the chapel and we're going to get maaaarrrrieddd!" I sang.

"Let's do it!" Love yelled, and Law lifted her into his arms. We left the room drunk and excited. We all went into the Jewelry store and Law told them to bring out the best and biggest diamond they had in there. This nigga spent damn near a million dollars on a ring for Love, and I almost fainted. Sin wouldn't let me see the ring he had gotten for me. Love and I picked out the rings we wanted the guys to have and we were on our way to the wedding chapel.

"Excuseee me, we want to get married allllll of us together!" I slurred, to the guy at the counter.

"Okay, I need for you all to fill out these forms and we will get you all married," the man told us. Once we filled the paperwork out, I asked the lady behind the counter to record the ceremony for us. About an hour later we were married, and we were hype as hell. Law and Love couldn't keep their hands off of each other. Sin and I were drinking and celebrating, I told everybody that passed by our ass. I was Mrs. Sincere Jacobs and Love was Mrs. Savion Williams, I couldn't believe it.

Chapter Twenty-Eight

SIN

"*B*abeeee, my head hurts," Tay groaned, poking me in my side. I was tired as fuck and I had the worse hangover. It's just a hangover, go in the bathroom and get two Advil's out my bag.

"Babe, I don't want to move," Tay complained, as her phone started ringing.

"Tay answer that annoying ass phone," I told her.

"It's Gabe calling me on facetime, I will call him back later," she said, and her phone started back ringing again. She grabbed it and answered the facetime.

"Hey, bro," she groggily spoke into the phone.

"I know damn well, y'all drunk ass niggas didn't get married!" Gabe said and then burst out laughing.

"Married!" both Tay and I yelled.

"Yes, married!" Gabe spoke.

"Nigga, we didn't get married. What the hell are you talking about, it's too early for your foolishness, bro," Tay told him.

"Girl you sent me a video, late last night talking about me and my husband this, and me and my husband that! Ohhhh, so you and your husband don't know that, that's your husband, huh?" He laughed, and Tay hung up the phone. She pulled up her text messages, and she damn sure sent Gabe a video! When she pressed play, I couldn't believe my damn eyes. We were down in some damn chapel, and all our asses had gotten fucking married!

"Ahhh, hell Nawl! Sin, what the fuck did we do?! This shit can't be fucking real! I know you forced me to marry you, while I was drunk. Fuck that, I want it back ion wanna be married to a crazy person. Ahhhhh hell the good dick alliance got me, and there is no turning back!" Taymar went on and on.

"Tay shut the hell up and let me think!" I grabbed my phone and called Law.

"Yeah," he answered.

"Bruh, are you and Love up?" I asked him.

"We are now, what's up?" he questioned.

"We will be right over there," I hung up, and ran in the bathroom to wash my face and brush my teeth. That's when I noticed the ring on my finger. Being married to Tay, wasn't a bad thing if I did do it. I would have liked to remember the shit though. Tay came in the bathroom talking to herself and pacing back and forth. This girl was fucking crazy, but I loved her crazy ass.

"Tay brush your shit, so we can go down to their room and figure this shit out," I said to her. We left the room and was now waiting for someone to open the door.

"Good morning, newlyweds," Love smiled.

"Ohhhh, nooo! It's true, and you look the fuck happy about it! Smiling and shit, like you done, hit the fucking jack-pot," Tay fussed.

"What?! You're not happy about being married?" she asked.

"We don't remember getting married," I responded.

"Ohhh, well I hate to tell you this. But we all are very married, and I'm so happy," Love said, just as Law walked in the room smiling.

"Please tell me y'all joking, right?" he asked.

"No, nigga we not joking. Y'all let us go and do the shit! Just because y'all happy go lucky asses was all for it. Doesn't mean we were ready to do the shit!" Tay yelled. "But you were ready Tay. You were singing and everything about you going to the chapel and getting married. You know that song, I thought it was so cute," Love laughed.

"You know sometimes, I wish I could just punch you in the damn throat," Tay told her. Both Love and my brother were bent over laughing so damn hard at us.

"I was drinking just as much as y'all and I remember every moment about last night. I knew that I wanted this beautiful woman to be my wife, and that's what we did," Law responded.

"Bruh, mom is going to kick our ass!" I said to him.

"She knows, I talked to her this morning. I told her why I wanted to do it, and she understood," he replied.

"We will call y'all later," I told them and pulled Tay out of the room. Walking back into our suite, I pulled her into my arms because she was really stressed.

"If you really don't want to be married to me. I will hire a lawyer to fix this and get us out of it. But I love you, and to be honest I'm feeling this shit. I'm really happy about it, I just want you to be happy about it as well."

"Are you serious, you want to be married to me?" she asked.

"Yes, I do," I replied, and she smiled.

"I love you too, babe. I'm just so shocked that we did something like that. I don't want you to feel like I don't love you. Because I do love you, and if you're happy and want to be in this for a lifetime, I want it to be in this marriage with you," she said, and I crashed my lips into hers. I pulled her in the bathroom and turned on the shower, as we stripped down.

"You know I never thought, that I would ever get to this point in my life. I'm ready for this shit, and I wouldn't want to do it with anybody else, but you," I said to her, pushing her up against the shower wall kissing her lips. Lifting her, as her legs wrapped around me.

I eased inside of her, and we both let out a moan.

"Relax, and let me take care of you baby," I told her, as I

moved in and out of her. She wrapped her arms around my neck tighter, as I gripped her ass spreading it further apart. I dug deeper, and deeper as I hit her spot over and over again. Tay was meeting my thrusts grinding her pussy into me, it was like something had taken over us.

"Give me that shit, baby! Fuck this dick," I growled, as I bit down on her neck.

"Mmmmm hmmmm, I'm cumming babe! Shittttt!" she screamed as we both came together. I couldn't believe that I had a wife, and I was loving this shit. Her ass was really stuck with me now.

Chapter Twenty-Nine
LOVE

*A*ll I could think about as my husband kissed and sucked while deep inside of me is that he was really my husband. We couldn't keep our hands off of each other. The way he was making love to me now even felt different.

"Fuck, I can't get enough of this pussy," Law growled, as he continued to thrust deeper, and deeper into my walls. I have never had dick so good in my life, this man was everything.

"Baby, ahhhhhh fuck, I have to.... mmmmmm," I moaned, it was so damn good I couldn't even form words.

"Let it go, lil' mama. Ohhhhh, fuck!" he roared, as we both released together. He pulled me into his arm and placed a kiss on my lips. I still couldn't believe that we were married, I felt like screaming that shit to the world. When he told his brother that he remembered everything about last night. He did, when I woke up this morning, he was staring at me. The first thing out of his mouth was that he should have married me years ago.

"Babe are you happy that we got married this way. I didn't even think about asking you if you wanted a big wedding. If that's what you want, I promise I will give it to you," he spoke.

"What we did last night was perfect, I only care about being your wife. I don't care about having a wedding, and bridesmaids. If I had a choice, I wouldn't change a thing about what we did. Hell, I would do it all over again, and it was kind of cute that we did it with Sin, and Tay," I told him.

"Yeah, that was pretty dope. It would have been cooler if they ass remembered the moment. Did you see Tay's face?" Law laughed.

"Yes, it may take her a while to actually come to terms that she's married," I said, as we continued to laugh about how Sin and Tay burst in our room this morning. Let's go shower and go out and get some lunch, Mrs. Williams," Law smiled, as we both got out of bed and headed for the shower. A few days had past and we were now back in Philly, at Ms. Naomi's house having dinner. We even had our Grammy here with us, and that made this moment so much better. "Love and Taymar you two did well. I love my grandsons, and I'm so happy for all of you. This really warms my heart to know that you all are married, and happy. That's all I ever wanted for you both. Law, and Sin I've known you boys since you were little boys running around with Love. Thank you both for always keeping her safe and helping me with anything that I needed.

I could never repay you for all that you've done," Grammy spoke, and Tay and I were in tears.

"Ms. Josephine, I saw your struggle and all of the sacrifices you made to make sure my wife was good. I saw you cry when Love got accepted into college and you knew you wouldn't be able to pay for it. I made a vow that day, that I would help you and make sure she went to school. I even came home and talked to my mom about it. You don't owe us anything, we love you, and thank you for allowing me to be a part of your family," Law told her, pulling her in for a hug.

"I'm so proud of my boys, y'all did good," Ms. Naomi said to them.

"Thanks, mom. I'm truly happy, and I love this woman with everything in me," Law said, and I smiled.

"This woman completes me; I swear, I never thought I would feel this way about a woman. But I love the hell out of my wife," Sin spoke.

"Awwww, I love you to baby," Tay told him. We sat around and talked for a while before we decided to go home.

"Dad, are you coming to play the game with me?" Savi asked his father.

"Yeah, go get it set up, and I will be right in there," he responded, and Savi took off. I can't wait until I have your son, he is so active and I'm so tired," I said to Law, as I started removing my clothes.

"I know baby we don't have much longer after I'm done with Savi. I will come in and give you a massage and feed you chocolate ice cream," he responded, and that made me smile because I loved chocolate ice cream. I saw that I had an email from my realtor down in Miami, and my house has a buyer. I was glad because the house has been on the market for about four months now. I had some interviews set up for a nanny for Savi, and the new baby next week. I planned to go back to work after the baby is born. I told Law I would stay home for about three months and then I was going back. I have been out of work long enough, and it was time to get back into the swing of things. I have been looking for buildings because I really wanted to open up my very own Pharmacy. A week had passed, and I haven't seen much of Tay she was so busy looking for office space for her marketing company. I called her on facetime and waited for her to answer.

"Hey boo," Tay spoke as she sat down at the table.

"Tay! I missed you, how is everything going?" I asked her.

"Girl, everything is good. I found the perfect location in Cheltenham for my business. I can't wait to get back to work, I can't sit home and look at Sin's ass every day," she laughed.

"I would love to look at my man every day, all day long, but I know that's not possible," I told her, and she gave me the side-eye.

"Girl I know we got bit by the alliance, but that nigga got you gone," she joked.

"That's how it's supposed to be. Tay, I have been on cloud nine, he's so attentive to my needs, and wants. Sometimes I have to pinch myself to make sure that it's real. We've fought so hard and been through so much shit to be together. I've learned to never make a life-altering decision, on temporary emotions. I just love everything about him, I'm so in love with that man," I told her.

"I'm so happy for you, I have always been team Law and Love," she replied. Life was good and I'm extremely happy. I have my husband, and my children to thank for that.

UNTITLED

Law

Four months Later

Today was my Birthday, and we were getting ready for my birthday party that Sin, was so hell-bent on throwing. I really just wanted to spend time with my close family and friends. Love was due any day now, and she hasn't been feeling well. But she said she felt absolutely fine and was ready to get out and have some fun.

"Babe, I'm ready but before we go, I have a gift for you," Love spoke, as she walked into the bedroom.

"Damn," I whispered under my breath. This woman made my heart skip a beat every time I looked at her.

"Hey handsome," she spoke kissing my lips.

"You look absolutely amazing, I love seeing you carrying a

life we created inside of you," I said to her.

"I love it too, but I'm ready to give his little ass an eviction notice," she smiled.

"Girl, leave my baby alone; he can come out when he's good and ready. Let's get out of here, and you've given me enough gifts today. What could you possibly have for me now?" I asked her, as we walked downstairs.

"Just one more gift, I promise, then we can leave. Savi daddy is ready!" she yelled out. Savi came running out of the family room with his nanny, Sonya behind him. He had a black scarf in his hand.

"Daddy you have to sit in the chair, we need to cover your eyes. We have a secret for you," he said, and we laughed.

"It's a surprise, baby, not a secret," Love corrected him.

"Same difference, mommy. We didn't tell him, which makes it a secret, and when he sees it he will be surprised," he shrugged, and I looked at Love.

"That's my son, he's so intelligent. He got all of that intelligent shit from his daddy," I laughed, and she nudged me in the shoulder. Savi wrapped the scarf around my eyes with help from his mother and they guided me outside.

"Okay, you can take the scarf off," Love spoke, and when I removed the scarf I laughed. My wife got me a Porsche Panamera, I have been looking at this car for months trying to decide if I would buy it or not.

"Ahhhhh man! Thank you so much, Babe," I spoke, pulling her in for a hug.

"Happy Birthday," she smiled, and I walked over to the

car. When I opened the door, I couldn't help but laugh. There were gift bags all over the car, I pulled a few of them out and inside were clothes, a new watch, and money. Love did to me what I had done to her years ago when I got her the car and filled it with gifts for her graduation. Something just crossed my mind, and I rubbed my hands across my face.

"Babe, I'm a Pharmacist with a doctoral degree, I make good money and everything I did came from those funds," she said to me, and I smiled. I guess she read my mind because I be damned if I was driving around in something his ass paid for. I know she was awarded the money in her settlement from Zion. But it just didn't sit right with me, it was her money and she deserved it. I just didn't want her to spend it on me, or my children. When it was concerning my family, I got all of that covered. I pulled the car into the garage; it was just too much stuff in it to drive tonight. By the time we made it to the club, it was a little after nine, and everyone was there having a good time. Even Gabe and his wife Gia came out to celebrate with us.

"About damn time, Love, we got you some apple juice, Sin said, as he handed me a drink.

"Happy Birthday!" Taymar shouted, giving me a hug.

"Thanks, sis," I replied.

"Happy Birthday, bruh!" Gabe stated, and his wife hugged me as well.

"Love, girl you look beautiful, I know you're ready to have that baby," Gia said to her.

"Girl yes, I can't wait," Love responded, and the ladies all went and took a seat.

"Happy birthday, baby boy!" My mom greeted me with a kiss on the cheek. She had her man Sean with her, and he was a pretty cool dude. Sin and I both liked him, and he loved our mom.

"Thank you, mom," I responded, as we joined the rest of the family.

"Happy Birthday to you," Sean said shaking my hand.

"Thank you, I appreciate that," I spoke, just as my mom pulled him away.

"Sin, isn't that, Taj coming our way?" I asked in surprise. Knowing that it was getting ready to be some shit.

"What the fuck?! How the fuck did she get up here?" he gritted.

"Hey guys, it's been a long time. How have you been, Sin?" she asked him.

"Married!" This dumb nigga said, and I burst into laughter.

"Married! You got married? Well what she don't know won't hurt her, I've missed you, daddy," she said, grabbing his hand, and Sin snatched away from her so damn quick.

"Bitch, who the fuck are you, and why the fuck is you grabbing on my husband?!" Tay yelled, which got the attention of my mother.

"Bitch! I got your bitch, bitch!" Taj yelled, and Taymar sent her fist crashing into Taj's jaw.

"Law hold my drink while I drag this hoe, bringing her messy ass up in here starting trouble!" My mom shouted, but the bouncers moved in quickly and pulled Taj out. Sin was holding onto Tay, and he seemed to have calmed her down. I shook my head because that could have gotten ugly real fast.

"Is she alright?" Love asked, walking up to me.

"Yeah, Sin, has it under control. How are feeling?" I asked her.

"I'm absolutely fabulous," Love stated, wrapping her arms around my neck.

"That's good...." she spoke but was cut off.

"Ahhhhhhhhhh!" she screamed as she began to crouch over holding her stomach.

"L, what's wrong?" I asked her.

"My water just broke, the baby is coming! Ohhhhhhh shit!" she screamed out, I picked her up and walked out. I could hear everyone screaming behind me, so I knew they were behind us.

"Yessss, we about to have a baby y'all! Sin is going to get the truck," Tay said. He needed to hurry the hell up, or I would be driving her myself.

"Bro, don't like ummm get to close when the baby comes out. I'm telling you now you gone always give your baby the side-eye when he does some questionable shit!" Gabe said, and Gia hit him. Love was screaming out in pain, and I felt fucking helpless right now.

"Where the fuck is, Sin?" I roared, getting pissed the hell off. I never wanted to see her like this.

"There he is," Tay shouted. When he pulled up, I slid my wife in the back seat and hopped in beside her. Tay jumped in the front, and my mother yelled that she was on her way. Sin shot out of the parking lot, and we made it to Jefferson hospital about twenty minutes later. Tay ran in to get help, while I pulled my wife out of the truck. Carrying her inside, they placed her in a wheelchair, and we were headed to labor and delivery. By the time they set her up and checked her out to see how far she had dilated. Love was ten centimeters and ready to push, the doctor came in the room.

"Mrs. Williams, I'm Dr. Myers, it looks like we're ready to push and your doctor won't make it in time. I will guide you through the entire process," he spoke, and I was scared out of my mind. She was in so much pain, and they couldn't give her an epidural to ease her pain. She had to have the baby naturally, and it was killing her. Tay and my mom walked into the room.

"What are they saying, son?" my mom asked.

"She's getting ready to push, and they can't give her nothing for pain," I responded.

"Ohhhh, fuck that! Like do they know that it's a human coming out of there! Dr. it's like a whole baby with legs and shit coming out of there. That lil' nigga might come out doing the Crip walk or something, and y'all not gonna give my cousin nothing for pain?" Tay questioned.

"Tay! It's fine, I just want to have the baby," Love cried.

"Bihhh! You crazy as hell! Yo ass over that looking like Kizzy from roots, and you talking about it's fine!" Tay fussed.

"Love I'm going to need you to push on the next contraction. Get ready and pushhhhh!" the doctor yelled, and she did what he told her to do.

"Okay, love, on the next one I need you to push as hard as you can, and we should have a baby. Here we go! Push!" he yelled. Love pushed, and my son came out screaming and crying.

"Ahhhhh hell nawl! What the hell is that all over him? Mmmmmm, mmmm, Sin not getting one of them, Ion care, I don't the hell care!" Tay yelled, and we couldn't help but laugh at her. I think she's scarred for life, and Sin was going to have to put up a fight to get her to have a baby. My son was everything, and the love I had for this woman was out of this world.

"Congratulations, he's seven pounds, two ounces, and twenty-one inches long. The time of birth was at 11:59 pm," the nurse stated, as they continued to check our son out and work on Love.

"Happy Birthday, baby, I guess I had one more gift to give you," Love whispered with a smile, and it hit me that she had our son on my birthday. We named him Omari Sincere Williams. Sin and I promised that we would name our first son after each other. But with my first son, it didn't work out that way. So, I wanted to give my second son a part of his name. Nothing could have prepared me for what I've been through in the last year. Life will throw you some curveballs, and I'm so happy that the curveballs were thrown my way. It redirected my walk in the path that God intended for me to have. The best gift I could have ever received is my children and the LOVE of my life.

I was so excited, today was the first day of business with my marketing firm. I already had a few clients under contract and was super excited about that. Being married turned out to be amazing, and we were so happy. Sin was the best husband and even though getting married came as a shock to our unruly drunk asses. We were having the best time, I loved everything about that man. Gabe and I got our dad squared away in a better living environment. My mom and dad were both surprised by the fact that I got married but they were both happy for me. Sin and I went down to see my mom last week and he got her wrapped around his finger.

We were all planning to take a family trip when Omari got a little older. He was soooo adorable and he looked identical to his father. Savi was a beautiful blend of both of his parents, but his brother had nothing of his mom. I needed to call and check on Love, it's been a couple of days.

"Hey, Tay, what's going on with you?" she asked.

"Nothing much, just working, today was the first day of business. Thank you so much for the flowers," I told her. She sent me this beautiful floral arrangement, and so did my husband. "No problem, it was just so you would know that I was thinking about you," Love spoke.

"So, did you talk to Grammy?" she asked.

"Yeah, I'm kind of sad about it, but I guess it's for the best," I responded. Grammy decided to move down to Virginia with my mother. She said that she wanted a change of scenery. My mom has been trying to get her to move down for the longest and she finally decided to do it.

"Yeah, I think she will be happier. Besides we will drive down and see her, it's not that long of a drive," Love stated.

"I guess you're right, I will be over this weekend to see y'all. I love you, boo," I told her, and we ended the call. By the time I made it home, it was a little after seven and Sin was already home.

"It smells good in here, what are you cooking baby?" I questioned, looking in the pots.

"I made a pot roast, and potatoes with gravy, girl," he smiled.

"What?! Babe you can't cook, where is my mother-in-law," I laughed, looking at his non-cooking ass.

"Okay, okay, she just left, she wanted to make sure you didn't have to cook tonight," he smiled, and I was cracking the hell up. My husband couldn't cook for shit, but he swore he was going to take the time to learn. My phone was ringing, and it was my brother calling me on Facetime.

"Hey, bro," I greeted him when his face popped on the screen.

"What the hell are you doing, you still married?" He laughed, he thought the way Sin and I got married was the funniest shit ever. He asked that damn question every time he called me.

"Hell yeah, we still married, nigga!" Sin yelled out.

"Nigga shut the hell up, that's why Tay cheated on you. She sent me that video too," Gabe laughed, and Sin appeared back in the kitchen snatching the phone out my hand.

"What fuckin' video?" he said with a mug on his face.

"I will sell it to you for a hundred G's, you're gonna want to see this shit. That nigga had nappy hair, and his name was Lenny!" Gabe told him laughing, and I almost coughed up a lung. He had Sin going until he mentioned the money. My brother was trying to get his money back for the truck he got me.

"Nigga get off my wife's phone," Sin laughed at his ass.

"Alright, I will talk to y'all later. Love you, sis," he said and hung up. The relationship between Gabe and I was so freaking awesome. We had the best time when we hung out, and I loved how he loved his baby sister.

"If it's one thing I'm sure of, it's that you would never

cheat on me. I love you, baby girl," he said wrapping his arms around my waist.

"I love you back, handsome." He kissed my lips, and for the rest of the night, we relaxed and loved on one another. I'm truly blessed and loved the hell out of my life, and my husband.

Chapter Thirty-One

SIN

One year later

"Sincere!" Tay yelled out; I was in my office wondering why the hell she was screaming like a madwoman.

"What's wrong?" I asked as I ran into the bedroom.

"Sin, I know damn well you didn't do this shit to me!" she fussed, as she paced back and forth talking to herself.

"Do what to you? Why the hell you talking to yourself like you crazy and shit?" I asked her.

"I know you didn't get me pregnant; I just know you fucking didn't!" she went on and on.

"Pregnant! Baby, are you having my baby?" I questioned, looking at her with the biggest smile on my face. Having my nephews were a blast but having my own child would be a blessing.

"That's what the hell this thing says, and I'm about to fuck you up! You didn't see what O did to Love when she had him. I don't have that type of pussy between my legs, to be having nothing like that," she spoke.

"How do you know that you're pregnant Tay?" I smiled at her.

"Don't fucking smile at me, I missed my period, I'm like six days late. I knew something was wrong because you know my bissshh be coming to visit right on time and we celebrate every time we see each other! But this month that hoe didn't show the fuck up! So, I knew something was wrong and I went to get a pregnancy test," she said and handed me the test. It said pregnant in the little box, my heart felt like it was going to burst. This beautiful, over the top, dramatic, sexy ass woman was about to have my baby. I grabbed my phone and sent my mother, and brother a text and our phones were ringing off the hook. Tay was on the phone with Love, telling her how she wanted to throw her whole body away. I just laughed at her, because she was so beautiful when she was stressed.

The next morning, she called her doctor to see if they could fit her in. We wanted to be sure that she was indeed pregnant when the doctor confirmed that she was about seven weeks. I had to catch her because her dramatic ass almost fainted. We were on our way home, and I had to make sure she was going to be alright.

"Tay, I want you to be happy about this. This is our child that we created in love, you don't want to have my baby?" I had to ask her.

"I do want to have your kids; I just didn't want to have to do the work. I thought we could ask Love to have them for us since we know her shit works well," she said, and we both burst out laughing.

"So, you were going to ask Love to be our surrogate?" I questioned her, still laughing at her ass.

"Hell yeah, she already tore her shit up! So, I was going to ask her to just let the doctor plant ours in her and have some for us!" She shrugged and was bent over laughing at her ass.

"Girl you crazy!" I told her.

"I know, but I want to have your babies, I was just shocked and nervous. This is our first time, and I don't want to mess up," she said.

"We're in this together, we won't mess up. Thank you for making me the happiest man in the world," I told her, as I pulled her hand to my lips. If this is what it feels like to be loved and to love someone so much you would give your life for theirs. I wouldn't change a thing about it, Taymar is all that I will ever need. Things worked out for the best for everyone, and we're truly blessed.

 he End

Made in the USA
Middletown, DE
05 May 2022

65338838R00106